For a Few Hours

For a Few Hours

Yvonne Walus

Bridge House

British Library Cataloguing in Publication Data
A Record of this Publication is available from the British
Library

ISBN 978-1-914199-20-2

This edition published 2022 by Bridge House Publishing
Manchester, England

Contents

Paradise for a Few Hours

What kind of woman hires a sex worker?

A stranger.

A woman like me.

Hello and welcome to another day in paradise. The time is 7.00 am and the air smells of home-cooked waffles.

"Just coffee for me, thanks." That's Ian, my husband. He's a big shot at an IT firm, and that's all I can tell you. There was a time when I could tell you what projects he managed, the names of his clients and colleagues, and what development environment they used. Just like there was a time when I had a career and deadlines and a life.

But now all I know is that Ian's a big shot in IT. More importantly, I know I'm a survivor.

"Just coffee for me, thanks," mimics my eleven-year old daughter.

"Eat your breakfast, Mia," I say, then do a mental cringe; exactly when did I turn into my mother?

Ian waves goodbye. We stopped kissing a long time ago.

My husband blames me. I blame the cancer.

Oh, he is still attentive enough at parties, the perfect ones we throw at our perfect house, or the ones we grace with our presence on other cliff tops. In public, he will stroke my thigh or drop a quick kiss onto my neck when everybody's looking. In private, he avoids bodily contact, as though the disease were infectious.

We're late.

I yell, I octopus schoolbags and sports gear into the car, then I speed-crawl through the school run. As though I were an ordinary mum.

Many women envy me my perfectly toned body, my perfect house, my perfect family. That's what I need; I need them to envy me. If they envy me hard enough, I may even start envying myself.

After my gym workout and a cigarette, I stop at a discreet white villa to have sex with a stranger. Today's guy looks like a model in his tight black jeans and the shirt he's left unbuttoned.

I strip – except for my tube top – and lie face down on the bed. No words; the advantage of paying for it. Soft music permeates the little room as he caresses sandalwood oil into my shoulders, buttocks and feet. Ten minutes later I turn onto my back and his fingertips print slippery circles into my stomach and thighs. He's been told not to touch my chest.

Any bloke would envy me my job. Every morning, I play hide-the-salami, and I get paid to do it. Doesn't get much better than that.

My rates dictate that all my clients are rich, and therefore finishing-school polite, preserved with creams and long days of leisure, with boob lifts and tummy tucks, with Botox or whatever the latest craze might be. What I like most is not the sex. I mean, sex is uber important when you aren't getting any, but regular sex is overrated.

No, what I like is the sense of power. My power to give or withhold. My power to fulfil their fantasies.

Every day, I enter my personal bit of paradise, where strangers worship my body with their money. They are lonely, lost, looking for love. I make them forget – for a few hours. Better than nothing.

Today's stranger looks healthy but one glance at the tube top and I know she's scarred – inside and out. I also know remission is not forever. My mum's lasted three years. When she died, my sister took it hard. Dad took it even harder; disappeared one fine morning, leaving me to look after Bronwyn. And that's what I've been doing: the best private school in town, extra lessons, horse riding, and ski camps. Just like the rich kids.

Easy money. Any bloke would envy me. And you know what? They bloody well should. A dream job. Paradise.

Back home, I'm still smiling as I start the dinner preparations. Ever since I got sick, we've had a cleaner three times a week and the garden services weekly, so I kill time by ironing Ian's business shirts to show him how much I love him.

Kill time… When the diagnosis came through, time was all I could think about. I wondered how much I had left. I counted every hour spent with and without the children. I renounced every activity I disliked, pruned out every time-filler, cut out TV and chit-chat lunches. My life post-diagnosis, the part that wasn't spent on treatment and recovery, was a blueprint for efficiency and time management.

And now? Now I even have time to colour coordinate the bathroom towels and bake Ian's favourite cake before it's time to chauffeur my children from school to drama and soccer and homework groups.

After school is where my two worlds mesh. Today's stranger from the discreet white villa has a younger sister in the same group as Mia. It's less awkward… than it should be; there is the surprise that comes from when you see somebody you know out of context, but I can handle that. Then he extends his hand to introduce himself – and I am ready for that too.

"I'm Damian, Bronwyn's brother, how are you?" As though we hadn't seen each other earlier this morning.

Before I have a chance to react, Mia launches into a lengthy recount of the last hour, including the announcement that she needs a pair of boots "the very same as Shelly's". And that is it.

Over her shoulder, I steal a look at Damian. Still the same tight jeans that sent electric shivers through me only five hours ago. Still the same shirt, now firmly buttoned up.

I reach into my bag for a cigarette.

His eyebrows lift. "Should you?" He reaches over and puts his hand on mine.

What I should be is furious with him for mentioning the unmentionable. Instead all I feel is tired. I shrug off his concern together with his fingers. Light up. Inhale.

"Mummy!" That's my son, who's not yet old enough to roll his eyes and call me "mu-um".

With that one word, I become a different person, a person who doesn't think about men in tight jeans, or sandalwood oil, or cigarettes.

"Let's go home," I hug him tight to what's left of my chest. By the time we're done cuddling, I've forgotten about Damian.

For the rest of the day, I'm a marionette, turning with every pull of the strings tugged by my children. Mummy-this, Mummy-that, Mum-do, Mum-help, may-I, why-not, I-don't-want-to-eat-carrots, Mum-come-here-there-is-a-big-spider-on-my-bookshelf, another-ten-minutes-Mummy-I-want-to-finish-watching-this.

Ian comes home when the children are already asleep. His eyes are wilted and there are stress lines in his jaw. He eats his dinner in front of the TV, though I will bet my factory-new BMW that he has no idea what he's watching. He gobbles up our anniversary cake on autopilot, without realising he's forgotten the date. Again.

By the time he switches off the TV, I'm in bed, sheltered by a set of chaste cream silk pyjamas.

And now he's under the covers, snaking towards me. "Come on, how about it?"

So much for foreplay.

9

I turn away. "You know why not."

"I can do you from the back. I won't see a thing."

And so much for sensitivity. *I can do you from the back.* Whatever happened to: *You are beautiful,* or: *You look even sexier with your boobs gone,* or: *Nipples are way overrated?*

"Goodnight, Ian."

"Women," he mutters. Then he raises his voice. "There is just no way to please you, is there? Look around you. You live in paradise. Any half-sane woman would love to trade places with you."

"Yeah," I bite back. "She would have to be only half-sane."

"Bitch!" He switches off his light and turns his face to the wall.

Throat constricted and eyes smarting, I desert the bed and slide out onto the deck. Out of habit, I reach for the cigarettes. I long for the burst of nicotine in my lungs, easing away the tension, ironing out the hurt. Suddenly I remember the look on Damian's face. His fingers on mine when he tried to stop me.

The kindness of strangers. I take aim and throw. The white-and-red packet makes a graceful arc through the evening air straight into the pampered clump of flax in the corner. My silver lighter inscribed "To my precious wife on our tenth anniversary" follows suit.

And then I climb back into the marital bed, pull the goose down duvet up to my chin, breathe in the faint lemon scent of my linen and the soap smell of the stranger I married.

So ends another day in my paradise. And I know that tomorrow will trace the same pattern in the cosmic makeup of my life. Still, I'm thankful for the hours of today, and I'm thankful that I was given tomorrow to look forward to. Some women without breasts aren't so lucky.

What kind of woman hires a sex worker?

10

One like me.

A stranger without boobs staring at me from every mirror.

_____

First published in *Hysteria 2* anthology, UK, November 2013

One Wedding and One Funeral

Pretoria, 31 July 1981

What Captain Trevor Watson wanted right now, more than anything in the universe, was to get laid. Go to a Ladies' Bar – stupid how South African law prohibited women from entering any other drinking establishment – chat up a chick, get into her panties, stifle his loneliness for a few hours.

Dream on. Most girls saved it for the wedding night, the way their mothers and grandmothers before them had, totally oblivious of the sex revolution sweeping through the rest of the world. But he could still hope, right? It was a bleak Friday evening, its dry cold drilling straight into the bone marrow, the way only a Transvaal winter chill could. Nothing on TV. No snooker invitations. Tickets to *Raiders of the Lost Ark* already sold out in every one of the three Pretoria theatres.

Only now, he had a corpse to deal with. A corpse – and a witness. Or was it a suspect? Christ, Watson hoped it was a suspect. With luck, he'd wrap this case in two hours, leave Jones with the paperwork, and get his arse to the bar. The pickings would be slimmer as the clock approached midnight, but also more desperate, easier to seduce. After a full-on week in the Murder and Robbery squad, he was done with hard work.

Except for...

He eyed the pale-green folder on his desk.

Shuddered.

Du Plessis had buggered off to Zimbabwe for a funeral, and left Watson to finish the investigation.

He'd rather gouge his eyes out than read another report. "Jones?"

"Yes, sir."

"Tell me about the case."

"A seventeen-year old white male, sir. Hans Swanepoel. A prefect at Pretoria Boys High School. Champion butterfly and backstroke swimmer. Academic over-achiever. A bit of a loner, reading between the lines, an Afrikaans boy in an English school, but nothing on his record to indicate any trouble. Shot dead with a .38 special Cobra. Took four bullets to the chest. Distance around a metre."

Watson raised his hand palm out, like a stop sign. Four bullets. Unusual. "How accurate?"

"The doc can't be certain of the order, but we have one bullet nicking the breastbone to the right, one going through the left nipple," Jones winced as he said it, "and exiting under the left armpit, the other two in the heart."

Not an experienced shooter, then. "Any luck with the gun?"

"Didn't find it."

"What about the witness?"

"Suspect, sir, according to Captain Du Plessis. Her name is Claudia Aberdeen. Also seventeen."

"Goes to the same school, does she?"

Jones gave him a blank face, which was the private's way of masking confusion. "Sir? She can't…"

"Kidding, Jones. Boys High – it's in the name."

"Yes, sir. Claudia goes to the Glen High. A co-ed school. She attended extra-curricular electronics classes with the victim."

"Other friends?"

"Nobody stands out. He sat together with his chess club at lunch. Between swimming, chess, electronics, and homework, he probably didn't have a lot of time to socialise outside of school."

"Right. So what happened?"

"On Wednesday 29 July, Prince Charles got married to Lady Diana Spencer."

Watson raised his eyebrow.

"It's connected, sir. You know how the ceremony was broadcast live on TV on Wednesday night? Claudia and Hans watched it together with his family at his house. Hans then walked Claudia back to hers, said hello to her parents, and set on his journey back home."

"On foot?"

"Yes, sir. He never made it back. His body was discovered the next morning – that's yesterday – by a domestic maid on her way to work. It was lying in the Agapanthus border of another house, about three hundred metres from the Aberdeens' home."

"Didn't his parents raise the alarm when he failed to return home?"

"His father is away on a business trip. His mother put his younger sisters to bed after the TV programme then fell asleep reading them a bedtime story. Didn't wake up until after midnight, went to bed assuming Hans was back in his room."

Had the whole world watched the bloody royal wedding apart from him? The last time Watson had switched on the TV was when McEnroe won Wimbledon a week earlier.

"We spoke to the maid who found the body?"

"Yes, sir. She's scared shi… out of her mind. Thinks we're going to pin this on her."

No bloody chance, Watson thought. Tempting as it was to point a finger and let the machine of injustice steamroll ahead, the case of the-domestic-servant-did-it-in-the-Agapanthus-with-a-gun simply didn't wash. Inter-racial violence hardly ever happened in Pretoria's South-East suburbs. The Pass Laws Act of 1952 required all black South Africans to carry

ID at all times, and those found in a white neighbourhood without a good reason were arrested on the spot.

This made the case both easier and more difficult. Easier, because the killer was probably somebody within the boy's social circle. More difficult, because Watson would not be thanked for putting a school kid in jail.

"What does Du Plessis make of it?"

Jones perked up. "His handwriting could rival a medic's, sir, but he did dedicate one whole sheet to write two words in capital letters, then underline them."

Watson raised his eyebrows.

"Sir, the words are *statutory rape*."

"And the girl is?"

"Seventeen. Of legal age."

"Let's go talk to this Claudia," Watson said. "Find out why Du Plessis is so keen to throw her in jail."

Miss Claudia Aberdeen lived with her parents and siblings in Silver Oak Street, a posh address in a posh suburb of Waterkloof. The street was lined with tall jacaranda trees – not oak trees as the name might suggest – and Watson knew that, come October, purple flowers would block out the sky above and carpet the kerbs below. On this last day of July, though, all he could see were bare branches in pools of yellow street lamps. Six pm and it was already dark.

"What plans went to the crapper for you tonight, Jones?" Misery loves company. Perhaps Jones had to throw away *Raiders* tickets, or cancel dinner with his girlfriend's family, or postpone a weekend in Sun City where gambling machines and blue movies were legal.

"No plans, sir."

Watson drove slowly, checking house numbers. "On a Friday night?" Hey, did Jones actually have a girlfriend? He looked too young, somehow, too soft.

15

"Yes, sir. I mean, no plans, sir."

They drove on in awkward silence. "Here's where the body was found," Jones said.

Watson drew to a halt, killed the headlights. Most gardens in this suburb had either side fences or hedges to demarcate the boundary lines between the properties, but no front fences to clash with the landscaped perfections of the front yards.

The garden where Hans Swanepoel had died was no exception, with a white picket fence running to the left and the right of it, and presumably at the back, but nothing in front bar a mass of tall flowering plants, sturdy enough to survive the cruel climate.

"Did the house owners hear the shots?"

"Yes, sir. They thought, in retrospect, that they may have heard something around ten, but the house is far away from the street, and all the windows were covered with heavy drapes against the cold. Do you want to interview them, Captain?"

"No point."

They got into the car and rolled forward three hundred and fifty metres, until they were parallel with the Aberdeen property. A few islands of complicated rockeries lined the street side of the garden, with a flat-stone path meandering to the front door. A flat-stone driveway led straight to a four-door garage, connected to the main house by an enclosed walkway.

The lady of the house answered the door, a petite blonde with creamy skin and lips so perfect that Watson felt a stab. *Thou shalt not covet thy neighbour's wife*, a Sunday School memory whispered to him. He grimaced, remembering how often he had done just that. And more than covet. He had followed through. Never regretted it.

"I'll get my husband," the blonde said before either policeman could greet her.

She led them through the soft beige foyer to the lounge, the fabric of her dress draping around her backside. "Bertie? For you," she said before withdrawing.

"Whisky, gentlemen?" Bertie Aberdeen suggested as soon as they sat down. "Brandy? Gin and tonic?"

Watson and Jones shook their heads in unison.

"Come on, don't let me drink alone on a Friday night."

"How about you have the whisky, Mr Aberdeen, while the private and I drink its companion? Soda on the rocks?"

"I mix my whisky with Coke, but I can get you a soda."

Watson did a mental eye-roll. No whisky, not even the cheapest blend, was bad enough to dilute it with Coca Cola. "Coke will be splendid, thank you," he said.

Icy glass in hand, he took Mr Aberdeen through the events of Wednesday evening. Mr and Mrs Aberdeen, it turned out, also watched the royal wedding together.

"Not that I bloody care about the monarchy." Aberdeen raised his own glass and took a large sip. "I just wanted to please the wife. She adores that Lady Diana. Plus, weddings always put her in an amorous mood, if you know what I mean." He winked. Actually winked.

Did this caricature of a man expect congratulations? Questions that would allow him to boast about his performance? Watson remembered Mrs Aberdeen's tight dress and bit down on his envy. "We know what you mean, sir. Did you see the boy that night? Hans Swanepoel?"

"He walked Claudia to the front door. Said goodnight to her, well and proper. Didn't stay for opsitkers."

Watson's Afrikaans was far from perfect, but he knew Aberdeen was referring to the old courting tradition, in which a candle would be lit at the beginning of the visit, and when it burned out, the suitor had to leave. Parents who disapproved of the suitor would provide a really short candle. Obviously.

"And had he stayed, how tall a candle would you have offered?"

For an instant, a grimace tightened Aberdeen's lips, only to be obliterated by the whisky glass. "Well, Captain, you know how it is. Seventeen-year old boys... do you have a daughter?"

Watson confessed that he didn't. Asked about the timing.

"I didn't look at the clock when they arrived, but it takes about twenty minutes to walk from the Swanepoels to here."

"And the wedding broadcast finished?"

Aberdeen shrugged.

"Nine," Jones supplied.

"So around nine thirty then?" Watson confirmed.

"Give or take."

"You didn't offer to drive Hans home?"

Aberdeen rocked his now empty whisky glass between his fingers. "Wife and I had a few drops while we watched TV. I know the law's lenient about drinking and driving, but to tell you the truth, I felt a bit sleepy."

Whisky combined with sex would do that to a man, Watson thought. Enough whisky would also make him a lousy shot, even from a distance of one metre. Aloud he said, "We'd like to talk to Claudia now, please."

Aberdeen's face hardened. Before he could protest, however, his wife materialised in the doorway. "I really don't think there is a need..."

"This is a police investigation, ma'am."

"So?" Hard. Protective. Like a leopardess with her cubs.

He resorted to the cliché borrowed from the silver screen. "So we can interview her here. Or take her downtown if you prefer."

The leopardess shot him a look. There were claws and teeth in that look. Probably the promise of blood to be spilled too. "In that case, I insist on staying while you interview her."

"Again, ma'am, I'm sorry. We need to see Claudia alone."

"She's still a child."

"She's seventeen, Mrs Aberdeen." *Old enough to have consensual sex*, he thought. *And if she had been a boy, old enough to go to the army and die defending South Africa from communists.*

Claudia Aberdeen was blonde and petite like her mother, but she lacked that certain something that made men like Watson stand up to attention. Pretty enough, but too unaware of her own charm, too innocent. Her eyes were puffed up and red. She shuffled into the lounge like a very old woman.

"We're sorry for your loss," Jones said. It was the first time he'd taken the lead in an interview, ever, and Watson sat up with surprise.

Then again, Claudia was – what – only three or four years younger than Jones. How old was Jones? Watson made a mental note to ask.

"I – Hans was just a friend." Claudia's shoulders hunched, as though shielding her from a gust of cold air. "We were just friends," she repeated. "We watched the royal wedding together, but that was all. Didn't Lady Diana look like a fairy-tale princess in that tiara? The whole wedding was like a fairy-tale. She must be so happy! She's married to the most eligible bachelor in the world."

The lady doth protest too much, Watson thought. *Just friends, my arse.*

Jones walked to the door separating the lounge from the foyer, and pulled it shut. Next he switched on the hi-fi. A record started spinning, and Jones manoeuvred the arm of the record player.

Watson watched the needle sink into the black grooves.

19

Now the night has gone, now the night has gone away, crooned a male voice. Watson remembered that the pop group was called *Air Supply. Doesn't seem that long, we hardly had two words to say.*

"So what really happened that night?" Jones suddenly sounded like a mixture of a best friend and a forgiving priest.

Claudia Aberdeen's eyes glittered. "He told me..." Her mouth widened and turned downwards. "He told me that he loved me." The next few words disappeared into her muffled sobs. She gulped, drew a few deep breaths. "Now I'll never get married. I'll never be as happy as Lady Di."

"So, to recap," Watson said on the way back to the police station. He'd let Jones take the wheel this time. The boy had earned it after the way he'd extracted the truth from the tearful teenager. "Claudia is all gaga over the royal wedding. Hans whispers a lot of sweet nothings to her, about two hearts beating as one, or some such nonsense..."

"Two hearts beating as one is Lionel Richie," Jones supplied. "His latest song, *Endless Love.* A duet with..."

"Yes, yes. Hans had the whole fairy-tale wedding, plus the twenty minutes it takes to walk from his house to hers, to spin the soulmates line and to promise eternal love..."

"Endless love."

"Very good. Endless. They do it in the garage, in her dad's precious *Dodge*, imported all the way from the USA. Beige leather seats, Jones, think about that. Your first time on beige leather. Must be pretty something."

Jones blushed all the way to the tips of his ears. "Sir, if I may. The first time is always special, beige leather or no."

Watson could think of several examples when the first time wouldn't be so special. Chose not to share. "True," he replied instead. "So imagine her dismay when the dirty deed is done, and it's all *bam-wham-thank-you-ma'am.*

Hans zips up his jeans. Claudia asks him to set the wedding date. And then Hans blackmails her. Tells her never to mention what happened or he'd have her arrested. Basically, pulls the old statutory rape trick."

According to the outdated letter of the law, the age of consent was sixteen for girls, but eighteen for boys – to cover the act of homosexual sex without actually mentioning it. Victorian etiquette for you. This resulted in two ironic twists. First, that seventeen was old enough to play soldiers, but not old enough to play hide-the-salami. And second, that a seventeen year old girl having sex with a seventeen year old boy was technically guilty of statutory rape. She'd never get prosecuted, of course, and any boy reporting such a crime would be laughed out of the police station, but Claudia had no way of knowing that.

"Captain. Do you think Claudia… did she… the gun…"

"Relax, Jones. Did you see how cut up she was? She's really grieving for that scumbag, and there's not a shred of guilt in her tears. Her father, on the other hand… Picture this, Jones. Aberdeen finishes 'paying attention' to his wife, and goes to the lounge to wait up for his daughter. What father wouldn't? And notice how he avoided telling us what time Claudia got home? He didn't want us to wonder what happened to the half an hour they spent in the *Dodge*."

Bloody impressive, Watson reflected.

Half an hour? Perhaps they did it more than once. Or perhaps Hans needed to coax her some more, quote the lyrics of yet another soppy ballad, before Claudia succumbed. "So Aberdeen hears them in the garage, goes in, sees his princess with her legs around a boy…"

"Wouldn't he shoot Hans straight away, sir? Or punch him in the head, pull him off his daughter somehow?"

Jones was right. Watson didn't have to be a dad to understand that much.

21

"The mom, though," Jones stopped for a red light. "I can see the mom."

Watson could see Mrs Aberdeen only too well, just not the way Jones did. He dragged his imagination out of the gutter where he and the lovely Mrs Aberdeen (what a pity he didn't know her first name) were having a fabulous time on beige leather, and stopped thinking with his other head.

"So you're saying Mrs Aberdeen waited up with her husband. She was the one who entered the garage and saw her daughter having sex, or heard the rape accusation. Hans walked Claudia to the front door, and she let her husband greet them while she went to get the gun. Notice how the Cobra, with its short barrel, is the type of weapon that would fit into a handbag. When Hans left, she ran after him. Called out to him, and when he turned around, she popped four bullets and left him to die where he fell."

"It makes sense, sir, doesn't it?"

It did make sense. Unfortunately for the lovely Mrs Aberdeen.

"So, are you going to order a search of the Aberdeen property?"

"Nah."

"But sir, the gun?"

"Is probably in Soweto. They've had two days to get rid of it. You don't seriously believe they would keep a murder weapon in the wall safe?"

"We haven't even interviewed Mrs Aberdeen, sir. She looks like the type who'd confess."

"That's exactly what I'm afraid of. Come on, Jones, hasn't her daughter suffered enough already? Claudia's boyfriend is dead, he turned out not to be the person she had thought he was, and she probably assumes she's damaged goods and no man will marry her. She doesn't need her mom in jail."

"Sir, with respect, the law…"

"…is not always right. And deserves none of your respect. Let's go, Jones."

When they arrived at the station, Watson filed a report. *Murder by person or persons unknown.* Then he took Jones out to a Ladies' Bar, where they chatted up two sisters while the jukebox was promising to keep on loving them.

Neither policeman managed to charm his way into any panties, but as July 31st gave way to 1 August 1981, Watson felt a sense of contentment wash over him. The communists were under control in Angola, that funny-looking Prince Charles got himself a gorgeous young wife, Claudia Aberdeen would have her mother around to help her get over Hans Swanepoel, and Hans's mother would never find out what a jerk she'd raised.

This was justice. Not as the law saw it, of course, but as Trevor Watson, Captain, knew it had to be delivered.

The Anthony Phase

Mum's in her Anthony Phase again. Means she's less of a mum and more of a moron. Like, she giggles every time he grabs her backside. Like, she lets him sleep at ours even though he stinks up the bathroom. Like, she spends the dole on makeup for her and beer for him, while the fridge stands empty.

"Mum." The hole in my stomach is as deep as Loch Ness. "Can me and Lucy go to Dad's for the weekend?" Dad smacks us with his belt if we're out of line, but at least he stocks up on cornflakes and milk and eggs. And on Saturdays, he always cooks breakfast: eggs and real meat sausages and onions fried so brown, they're both sweet and bitter at the same time.

Mum puckers her brow to help her decide. She's in the beginning of a new Anthony Phase, so there are still things she finds more important than having the house to herself. "No," she says, her hand slapping the countertop for emphasis. "It's not Dad's turn to have you."

That's why I take the English teacher's money. Honestly, she should know better than to leave it in her coat pocket. Where does she think she works, Archangel High? After school, I pick up Lucy from her primary and we feast on fried chicken and chips from the local shop before we head home, to Mum and Anthony. It's only just begun, and I already can't wait for the Anthony Phase to be over.

As soon as we enter, Anthony's hog eyes, small and mean and eyelash-less, zoom in on Lucy. I can only see her back, but I remember her mouth is still shiny from the chicken grease.

"Hey, you." His finger, short and grimy, zaps her in place. I can't see her expression, but her shoulders are pulled tense. "Yes, you, Missy. Since when do you wear lipstick?" Anthony heaves himself off the sofa and I watch the dirty finger approach, closer and closer to my baby sister. It's less than an inch away, when I take a step forwards, push past her. "Sorry, Luce." Hoping she'll get the hint and run.

No such luck.

I'm staring straight into Anthony's broad chest. He's not wearing a shirt and I get an eyeful of the freckly vampire-white skin, the sparse ginger hair between his nipples, a moist orange mop peeking from under each armpit. My nose conjures up all kinds of foul smells trapped in the chalices of those armpits. The fat-drenched chicken in my stomach is threatening to cluck up.

"Go see Mum, Lucy," I throw the words over my shoulder like a safety net, my eyes still on Anthony. "Think I heard her call."

Lucy is just standing there.

"Lucy, for fuck's sake." I never swear at her, and now it gets me the result. Lucy makes a lost baby sparrow sound and legs it to the kitchen.

That leaves me eye-level with Anthony's armpits. The way to handle bullies, like 99% of the time, is to bully them right back, because they're total cowards. You stand up to them, and they fold at the first sign of strength. I lift my chin to look square into those hog eyes. My voice comes out a seventeen-year old growl. "You leave my sister alone."

Anthony falls into the other 1%. He punches me in the gut. Even though I remember to tense my muscles, his fist torpedoes through my defences and finds its mark. I fold in two, roll on the floor, my lungs starved for air. When I finally manage to breathe in, it's like I have to suck five times as hard as usual.

"Want me to sock you another?" Anthony asks.

25

He wants me to cower. Plea. Grovel.

I do all three. Hey, I'm not proud of it, but schoolyard fights haven't prepared me for one grown-up clout sweet into the solar plexus.

"Glad we sorted that out." The smirk makes the humiliation worse. "You know, Lucy wouldn't want us to clash. Lucy..." He repeats her name slowly, rolling it in his mouth with plenty of tongue showing. His hand accompanies his words in a series of obscene gestures.

I want to kill him. Instead, I slink off to puke streams of liquid fried chicken into the toilet bowl. At night, instead of dinner, we get served news.

"You won't believe it!" Mum's eyes are bright like after a joint. "Me and Anthony are getting married!"

Planning to get married is one of the steps in the Anthony Phase. Step one: forgive and fornicate. Step two: move in. Step three: plan to get married. Step four: break up before they get their shit together.

"In Majorca," Mom squeals. "Next month!"

The Majorca bit is new. Lucy runs up to Mum and they form a female knot of hugs and chuckles and words like "confetti". I don't understand Anthony's puffed up air of triumph – after all, Mum's already got divorced once, she can do it again – until Lucy throws herself at me shouting, "I'll be the bridesmaid, I'll be the bridesmaid!"

"Sorry, mate," Anthony says to me in a not-sorry tone. "Only had money for three tickets. You're staying home." He grins his arse-ugly grin. "Throw a party. I'll leave you a pack of beer if you behave." Meaning, if I let Luce go to Majorca without a fuss.

My stomach remembers the liquid chicken and churns. I swallow the gastric reflux burning the back of my throat. I don't need Anthony to draw me a picture. Mum's a sound sleeper, especially after a drink or two, and with her out of the picture, Lucy's on her own with Anthony. Bastard thinks I'll trade my sister for a fridge full of booze.

Shit.

Don't know how to stop him.

Have no plan.

Want to kill him.

Fate provides me with a potential weapon, when I break into one of the posh houses on our way to school. The owners drive hybrids and there's a spa pool in the garden, so they're doing all right, while Lucy needs money for her school camp. There's a school hardship fund she can apply for, but I don't want her to. Bad enough she gets lunch out of the PTA freezer, a donated bread roll with a smear of cheese spread. You know, if you go through the humiliation of asking for charity, it's insulting not to be given a nutritious meal, with fruit and a glass of milk. So the school can go screw itself with its goodwill. I'll get Lucy the camp money myself.

I wriggle a bit of wire in the back door of the rich couple's house, ignore the blaring of the alarm, and within minutes I'm the proud owner of an iPod, two laptops, a figurine of a naked chick riding a lion (looks like silver) and a yellow taser gun. I know it's a taser because a couple of policemen came to our school last year to talk about joining them as a career, and to tempt us they showed us their truncheons and taser guns.

Shit. This guy is either a cop or has taken the gun off a cop. I don't hang around to find out. Five seconds after pocketing the gun, I'm out of there, across the hedge, up the hill and safely inside Lucy's school perimeter just as the street below reverberates with the screech of a security van.

I wave to Lucy across the soccer field to let her know all's well. Decide to skive off school to sell the stolen goods. The taser I keep, thinking up the various ways I could apply it to Anthony's body parts. A fence I know from previous transactions pays for the rest of the loot, the electronics and the porn lady. It's peanuts. Still, the money covers Lucy's camp, with enough left over for dinner. Lucy says Macdonald's meals are rubbish, but I can't picture eating fried chicken anytime soon.

At home, there's no sign the Anthony Phase may be nearing its end. He and Mum are at it like rabbits every chance they get. Still, there's this worrying incident with the bathroom door. The lock breaks mysteriously one day when we're at school, and Anthony promises to fix it. Course, he never does.

Twice, he walks in on Lucy when she's showering. We have no curtain. Lucy freaks. Mum tells her off for parading naked in front of her, Mum's, boyfriend.

I take to hanging round the corridor whenever Lucy's in the bathroom.

"You little perv," Anthony says when he collides with me in the small space by the bathroom door. "Checking out your sister's tiny tits?"

That's what he calls them. Tiny tits. And he makes that wanking gesture again. I wish I could spew fried chicken all over his face.

At school, the homeroom teacher asks me what I plan to do with my life. Says I could be a business writer, a journo, a novelist. Apparently I have talent. Ha! I'd trade in my talent for the end of this Anthony Phase any day. Wish my talent lay in getting rid of people. I wonder if a taser gun can kill.

When Lucy leaves for school camp, I breathe easier. Mum lets me stay with Dad, even though it's not his turn. The Anthony Phase must be well under way.

"I don't like Anthony," I tell Dad on Night One. We're watching the sports channel and eating takeaway pizza. Just

28

like back home, it's always the man of the house controlling the TV but at Dad's at least we get to eat.

Dad shrugs, says nothing.

"Creeps me out," I try again. "Much rather live with you."

Another shrug.

"Can we, Dad? Move in with you? Me and Luce don't mind sharing a bedroom."

"Speak to your mother." Which is his way of saying no.

"The way he treats Lucy," I try again. Hesitate. How do you begin to explain sexual abuse to your old man?

Dad doesn't get it. "She talks back, she needs to be taught respect."

Urgh!

The day Lucy returns from camp, I go back home. Mum is still wearing a lot of makeup but at least she's back being Mum.

"Kicked Anthony out, I did," she tells us. "Bloody control freak."

I spot a cut lip and a silver swelling on her cheekbone under all the face paint, but I know better than to hope the problem solved. A week before their trip to Majorca, Anthony is back with a spray of long-stemmed roses and a diamond ring.

And so begins a new Anthony Phase. Mum buys Lucy swimming togs for the trip. My pit of despair is growing deeper by the hour.

"Weird to take your daughter with you on your honeymoon," I tell Mum.

"You're just jealous you're not going."

The pit of despair deepens some more.

The night before they fly out, I give Lucy the taser gun. "If he ever tries anything with you…"

She laughs me off. Chucks the gun onto the stack of empty

banana boxes that is her nightstand. Refuses to pack it. "What on earth can he do to me?"

I don't tell her. I can't. For somebody supposedly so good at writing, I have no words.

A few hours later, I wake up and she's standing there. It's 2 am, her pyjama top is unbuttoned, and her teeth are banging together. In the distance, I hear Mum's snore, the loud one, the one that heralds she's had a few hard drinks and is now dead to the world till noon.

"Luce!"

I drape my blanket around her. Hold her for long, long minutes. Fetch a glass of *Coke*. Her lower lip bumps into the glass in a wooden attempt to drink. A few drops of the brown liquid stain her white PJs. Like blood.

"Tell me."

She shakes her head.

My mouth filling with dread, I go inspect her bedroom. Anthony is sprawled across Lucy's bed, face buried in her pillow, bare butt pointing up. The ginger hairs on his buttocks are not as sparse as the ones I remember on his chest. His usual stink is amplified tenfold.

No need to touch him. I know he won't be getting up. Ever. The yellow of the taser draws my gaze to the floor. Lucy must have grabbed the weapon off her stack of banana boxes. From the position of the body, I can't tell whether he was still standing when she zapped him or whether his weight was already over her. It's important. Shit. I'll have to guess. No way am I asking her.

I walk to the bed, careful not to touch the suffocated bulk that used to be Anthony. Pick up the taser. Wipe off Lucy's prints.

When I get back to my own bedroom, she's still sitting there, blanket across her shoulders, stare empty of life.

"Look at me, Luce."

She does, but her eyes remain blank.

"You didn't do it. I did. I went to piss and heard you calling for help. Get it?"

I repeat it into the phone when I call emergency. I keep Lucy with me and tell it again to the uniforms who arrive on the scene. When they say I have to go with them and Mum can't be roused, I dial Dad's number and tell the story once more time. Perhaps the repetition will sink in. Perhaps it'll even convince Lucy she's mis-remembering what really happened.

So, I get my wish. The Anthony Phase is over. For ever. My new dream is that the prison cell's warm, that they serve three big meals every day and that I get to control the communal TV remote while awaiting my day in court.

Not a grand dream, I grant you that. Beats being a writer, though.

The Father-Daughter Club

The first rule of the Father-Daughter Club is you do not talk about the Father-Daughter Club. The second rule of the Father-Daughter Club is you *do not* talk about the Father-Daughter Club. It's okay to talk about the daughter though.

That's why I do it.

All the time.

"How can I help you today?" The sales girl at the cosmetics store is bubbly, and her tone implies that selecting the best product to suit my needs will totally make her day.

I use my opening smile, which makes me come across baffled and slightly embarrassed. "It's my daughter's birthday this weekend and I'd like to buy her some bath bombs or whatever it is girls like."

"Wow, happy birthday to your daughter! How old? Is she more of a tomboy or a princess?"

The conversation flows easily, and soon my shopping basket is filled with citrus-scented soaps, coffee body scrubs and bath bombs guaranteed to turn the water into liquid gold. I even buy a natural shampoo bar that doesn't need a plastic bottle ("so environmentally-friendly!") and chocolate-flavoured lip balm ("because all teenagers love lip balm").

"Can you gift-wrap each item separately? My daughter loves opening presents."

I pay cash, asking for change in ten-dollar notes, and walk out of the shop with a spring in my step and the sales girl's contact details in my phone. Friday lunchtime well spent.

On the way back to work, I pass four homeless men, and I give them each a tenner. Ten bucks will buy two coffees, or two big burgers with fries, or a hit of whatever they need to make their lives bearable for a few hours. Who am I to judge?

"Weekend plans?" asks a colleague when we queue up for the water cooler in the office kitchen. Mary-Lou has teenage children of her own, so I have to tread carefully.

"Not much. Pizza and movies with my daughter tonight. Chauffeuring her to a netball game and drum lesson tomorrow."

"How old is she now? Soon she'll have her licence and there'll be no need for you to do all that driving."

I nod and change the subject. "How about you? What are you up to this weekend?"

While she prattles on about a campervan trip, I make a mental note to browse the job ads. Looks like I've stayed with this crowd too long.

Back home, I kick off my shoes and pull off the necktie.

"I'm home," I call out, though I don't expect an answer. Sprawled on the sofa, I dial one of the numbers in my Star Contacts. "A pepperoni pizza for me, and a vegetarian one for my daughter," I tell the guy who picks up the phone at the local pizza shop.

The wine bottle opened to breathe and the bath products put away in the cupboard, I browse the movie options while waiting for dinner to be delivered to my doorstep. This is the good life. If my daughter were here, we'd probably argue about which show to watch, so it's just as well that I'm alone.

Later, much later, I fall into bed and close my eyes without switching on the alarm. Nowhere to be in the morning except right here.

The first time I invented my daughter was fifteen years ago. My first job, a few months in, I was asked to work over the long weekend. Normally, I would have agreed, but I had already booked a romantic get-away, and as my then-girlfriend was going hot and cold on me, I needed the opportunity to figure out what was what. Using an engagement ring, no less.

Plus, the project was super-boring.

"I'm so sorry," I said, pulling my mouth into a disappointed grin. "Would love to, but I need to look after my baby daughter. Her mum," I broke off, mumbled something. "Anyway, she's out of the picture for now. And my parents live in England," that last bit at least was true.

"Oh, wow. I didn't realise you're a solo dad," my boss touched my shoulder, the briefest of contacts, but a major barrier broken. "You should have mentioned it."

If I were a mother, a woman who tried to use her child as a reason not to work on a Saturday, I would have been deemed less-than-professional and not fully committed to my career. A man, though – what a bloke!

Unfair, I know. I felt bad. Then I felt even worse when I got dumped while on one knee holding up a diamond ring. Thinking back, perhaps it was karma. Or maybe Abigail – the only woman who'd ever made me want to settle down – simply wasn't that into me.

The feeling of guilt at the office was amplified when I got promoted to a team leader position, because – as a father – I'd be a good fit for the role. The irony being, not many mothers hear that their parenting skills make them a natural manager.

So yes, it's all super-unfair and super-unethical. But to paraphrase a great modern philosopher, we are all slaves with white collars chasing after cars and clothes, working jobs we hate so we can buy stuff we don't need. We are rats running in never-ending mazes, consuming the world and producing nothing in return except excrement.

Think about today's jobs – not nurses and builders, of course, for they supply meaningful services – but all the middle managers and senior managers, the data crunchers and advertisers. How many of them could disappear tomorrow, leaving the fabric of our society completely intact?

I'm a bureaucrat working for the government. Yes, your taxes pay my salary. And if I stopped delivering my projects tomorrow, you wouldn't be any worse off. Chances are you wouldn't even notice.

Saturday night, the gift-wrapped shampoo bar in hand, I arrive at my current girlfriend's apartment. Okay, one of my girlfriends. "Happy one-month anniversary," I tell her as I hand her the present.

Tanya is an environment fanatic so the idea of shampoo without a plastic bottle is an instant hit. We are consumers. No matter how careful Tanya may be about plastics, she's still into material things. And your possessions end up possessing you.

That's why I choose to own little and to invest in living life to the brim.

"You must be exhausted after a whole day of child-minding," Tanya says. She thinks my daughter is five. "Tell you what. Instead of going out, why don't I whip up a Thai omelette, while you relax and watch TV?"

I pull her close. "Sounds like heaven." It's the truth. I love home-cooked meals, but it's always too much bother to prepare dinner for one. "Forget the TV. Let's talk."

I get enough TV at home. The main reason I date multiple women is not what you think. I mean yes, the sex aspect is fantastic. The main reason, though, is the company.

Lame? You bet.

"Can you stay till morning?" Tanya asks after we've eaten.

Nothing better than waking up with someone I like after a night of hiding the salami. Unfortunately, I don't like Tanya that much, so I make a sad face and check the time. "The babysitter needs to go home at midnight."

"We'd better hurry up, then," she says as she dims the lights.

Sunday morning the weather cooperates, so I take my bike for a 30 km outing along the beach, across the bush, up and down and through the mud. Get home sweaty, dirty, muscles aching, and adrenaline buzzing. If I had a daughter, I'd be watching cartoons with her, or shopping for makeup, or helping with maths homework. Instead, I shower until the hot water runs out, then text the girl from the cosmetics store.

We're getting drinks on Tuesday.

The drinks go better than expected, and I'm still exhausted the next morning, so I take sick leave. "It's my daughter. Only a sore throat at the moment, but she has a temperature, so I have to keep an eye on her." So much easier than faking a cold myself – just blame it on my child. The problem is, my child is growing up, and so I need a change of scene.

During the interview for my new job on Thursday, I mention my daughter right away. Important to check whether they'd be as understanding as my current employer. They are. My potential boss congratulates me on my honesty. "So many parents avoid talking about their families," she says. "I believe you will be a great addition to the team. How old is your daughter?"

"Five." That should give me ten years with this company before my imaginary daughter gets too old to be useful.

"That's such a cool age. At school already?"

Thinking on my feet, I dig out my old knowledge of five-year olds, share a few anecdotes. "She can count already," I pretend-brag, "but I haven't started teaching her to read. The school can do that. Wouldn't want her to get bored and start acting up."

As soon as it's polite, I turn the conversation back to my new job.

"Your opposite number in Communications will also be a new appointee," the new boss says, "so the two of you will bring fresh enthusiasm and perspective to the project. You'll work closely together to create opportunities..."

I stop listening.

That night, after sex, Tanya brings up the taboo topic. "I'd like to meet your daughter sometime."

That's my exit cue. Done it so many times before, I have the speech memorised: my daughter and I belong to an exclusive club of two. I allow myself a social life which has to be totally separate from my family life. I won't ever let myself be distracted by having emotions for anyone else, and I can't risk my daughter ever getting close to a woman who will break her heart when she stops dating her dad. Over the years, I've kept this part deliberately confusing (who is dating whose dad?), and it always works.

Tanya cries, I say nothing needs to change, and that we can continue dating. Alas, Tanya wants more than dating, so even though we both promise to call soon, we know this is goodbye.

The new job is all go, so I give my notice at work. "My daughter's excited about this development," I tell them, hoping to get a laugh. "Her school is on the way to the new office. I'll be able to drop her off in the morning."

Mary-Lou, the colleague who has teenage children, takes me aside.

"This is still confidential, but I'll be joining your new company as the Head of Communications," she says. "Not sure when, I have to tie up a few loose ends here, but I'll definitely be there for the Family Christmas Party."

"The what?"

"Oh, didn't they tell you? Their social club runs events for the whole family, children and teens included. I look forward to meeting your daughter at long last."

As soon as I get home that evening, I head straight for the drinks cabinet. *Lagavulin* is my first love, a somewhat rough introduction into the bed of single malts: smoky in the extreme, its first kiss is always arrogance before it suddenly melts into honey.

Three whiskies later, I'm still no closer to solving the Mary-Lou problem, when the doorbell rings. The living room sways ever so slightly as I traverse the carpet to answer the door.

A young person is standing on my doormat. Short hair with a purple fringe that covers most of the face. A gold stud in the nose, like a pimple full of pus ready to be squeezed. Laddered jeans, one hole so big you can see the knee.

It looks up at me. Female. Something familiar around the jawline. Eyes the exact replica of Abigail's, hard like the diamond I tried to give her all those years ago.

The girl swings her backpack into my limp arms.

"Hi, Dad," she says.

Two Chairs at the End of the Road

Every day my husband stands by the window and waits for the postie.

"She's not here yet," he says.

"It's too early," I reply every day. "She'll be here soon."

Before my husband retired, he was a financial auditor, his brilliant brain responsible for multi-billion accounts. Now his brilliant brain calculates the minutes left until his daily handful of junk mail and bills.

He likes the bills. He's never taken to e-commerce, so he pays them by cheque and enters the amount in the Household Expenses spreadsheet.

I want to scream. This is not what I imagined retirement would be like. This is not what I imagined marriage would be like.

As a bride almost half a century ago, I imagined that starry-eyed feeling would last us a lifetime. Turned out all those romance books and movies were a fairytale.

Retirement is a different type of a fairytale, one straight out of a book of Brothers Grimm horror stories. When my husband and I moved from a multi-level house on a hill in the suburbs to a one-level townhouse overlooking a quiet street in Nowhereville, we planned to use the money from the downgrade to see the world.

Ha! What the *How To Be A Sucker* books don't tell you is that if you work hard and pinch pennies all your life, you might not have enough life left to enjoy the pounds you've saved. In my husband's case, it is *not enough health left*. His blood pressure prohibits all travel and most excitement.

"The garbage collection is here."

We moved to a place with a short and flat driveway, so that we wouldn't have to cart the rubbish up and down the driveway. The trade-off is that we get to watch the bag

39

swing into the loud, stinky mouth of the waste disposal truck. Sometimes I think that for my husband it's a bonus rather than a trade-off. When excitement is prohibited, you make it where you can.

"The Taylors put out two bags again. I wonder what it is they're throwing away."

What are they throwing away? *Their lives.* One empty tin of baked beans after another.

The Taylors are just like us: retired and bored. On Wednesday mornings, they come over for a cup of coffee (decaf) and a biscuit (digestive). On Fridays, we trot over to theirs for afternoon tea.

Life in the fast lane, not, as our grandson would say. He doesn't visit often.

A streak of post-office-red flickers through the bushes. My husband watches it with the concentration he used to reserve for soccer matches and white-collar crimes. Always worried that the postie would skip us one morning, he exhales with relief when the bike stops at our gate.

"I'll go get it, shall I?" he asks, the way he did yesterday and all the days before. He used to ask important questions, like *is this Big Name company cheating our country out of tax money*? Now he asks about the post.

"Please."

I used to be a scientist, asking important questions about whether soy is bad for infants and whether food additives cause ADHD. I used to be a mother, asking whether my boring suburban life was the way to go. Now I ask my husband to bring in the bills and the junk mail.

The phone rings in the hallway when he is halfway to the box. It's not a big distance, but he doesn't react to the sound. It's not the first time I notice his hearing is that of an old man. My heart hurts for him.

"Hello?" I say into the phone.

40

"Mum?"

Who else would it be? The Tooth Fairy?

"Hello, Deborah. How are you, honey?"

"Mum, don't freak."

I'm freaking already. *Count to ten, grip the edge of the table, swallow.* "Okay. I won't."

"I'm getting a divorce."

My head is spinning, and I sit down on the floor. We must put a chair here. "But…" I begin.

"Hear me out, Mum."

But I stayed with your father for forty years so that you and your brothers would have a role model, I want to say. *But I didn't run off to Paris when I had the chance. But I didn't follow my heart and it was the right decision. But when you're my age you'll realise what marriage is and what marriage isn't…*

"Sure, honey." I tell my daughter. My grown-up irresponsible daughter. "I'm listening."

"I don't want to turn into you, Mum. Sorry if it sounds harsh."

It sounds harsh. "There are worse things in the world than being me."

"There are better things, too. I want to see the world, Mum. Howard is stifling me. He's just like Dad."

I glance through the window. Her father is standing by the yellow picket fence, envelopes in hand, talking to Mrs. Taylor. Sometimes I wonder whether she, too, waits at the window every day. She certainly seems to be in the garden every time he goes out to fetch the mail.

In all the time we've been married, I never had any reason to worry about the Mrs. Taylors of Temptation Street. My husband has values and he sticks to them, blind to any opportunities of having his bit on the side. I envy him that. And I love him all the more for his simple integrity.

41

"Don't knock your Dad, Deborah. There are…"

"…worse men in the world. Got it, Mum. I'm going to Torremolinos with a better one, though."

Torremolinos. Paris. History repeating itself: same choices, different outcomes.

What would my life have been like had I chosen Paris? Deborah wouldn't have been conceived, for one, and today she wouldn't be here to follow a different path.

Fate.

Quantum physics.

Fluke.

"I hope it works out for you, honey."

"Hope it works out for you, too, Mum."

What does she mean, *hope it works out for you, too*? She doesn't know about the man who almost took me to Paris. She doesn't know how close she'd come to not being. She will never know how close I get every day to question the point of my marriage.

When my husband walks in the door, my hands are not shaking and my lips are smiling. He'll never know how close I get every day to question the point of our marriage either.

I look at his tired face, his smiling lips, his loving eyes. He's happy in our marriage, our retirement, our life. That makes one of us. That's enough. No way am I telling him about Deborah's decision. Not yet, anyway.

"Coffee?" I ask.

"That'll be nice." His stock answer, measured and predictable.

"Did we get any mail?"

He waves the white envelopes, his face almost animated. "Four letters today."

I start the kettle. "Anything other than bills?"

"One bill, two appeals for charity, and a *Reader's Digest* offer."

He opens the envelopes on the sofa, visibly savouring the process of inserting the knife under the flap, slicing through the paper fold, unfolding the sheets.

Thirty years ago, dealing with the mail was a chore. We'd dump it on the hall table, and on a Sunday night one of us would sit down with the chequebook and the wastepaper basket, bickering whose turn it was, and that life was a bitch.

We had no idea.

"Here's your coffee."

He takes a sip, scowls. "Low-fat milk."

I could tell him to complain to the GP, except that Deborah's phone call has made me remember.

The guy who wanted to take me to Paris was the total opposite of my husband. Unreliable, unpredictable, always full of surprises. The most exasperating man I had ever known. The most exciting one, too.

When I told him I wouldn't walk away from my two sons, he cried. Promised that when I was done playing happy families, he'd come back for me. He'd build a small house with one bedroom and two chairs on the porch. "Chances are we'll be too old to have sex by then," he said, and his eyes were pure fire. "We'll spend the rest of our lives sitting on the deck talking about how good it could have been."

I wonder whether he's built the house.

I wonder what sex with him would have been like.

I'll never know.

What I do know is this. If I were sitting with him right now, on a porch big enough for only two chairs, I would not be serving coffee with low fat milk.

I take my husband's still full cup from his hand.

"Let me make you a fresh batch. With sugar and cream, the way you like it."

He doesn't ask unnecessary questions. "That'll be nice." Prudent, peaceful, predictable.

He never promised me a house to grow old in. He simply made it happen. That's marriage. Not a fairytale. Something better than a fairytale.

I hesitate. It's hard to let go of one's dreams. "Perhaps we could go shopping after lunch."

His eyebrows meet in confusion. "You always do the groceries on Tuesdays."

"It's not groceries. I'd like to buy some chairs. Two outdoors chairs for our porch."

Tomorrow, we'll sit outside with cups of creamy coffee and wait for the postie together.

Revenge of the Redhead

It didn't matter that he was brilliant in maths. Nor that he scored the most goals in hockey. All that mattered was that his hair was the ugly hue of cooked pumpkin. He was always *Flame Brain* or *Ronald Macdonald*.

His twin sister had better luck with *Fire Bush*. Her hair did look like a shrub on fire, though that was not what the local boys meant.

The idea must have originated with his sister's teen pregnancy, evolved during a series of his own unsuccessful first dates.

Redheaded girls were hot, redheaded guys were not. Time to change the world.

He ticked all the boxes: over 20, healthy, nice personality. His soldiers were valiant and thawed well.

Within a year, the clinic informed him of ten successful births, the maximum limit allowed in New Zealand.

He booked a ticket to the USA. Painting the world's hair red, one country at a time.

Pills of Perfection

The pill looks like a miniature blue pillow, a rounded diamond shape with Pfizer embossed into its convex surface. Pretty. Totally unfamiliar.

I'm on a first-name basis with pills. Every morning, I swallow a cocktail of thyroid hormones (a tiny round white tablet), multivitamins (a beige oblong pill), appetite suppressants (a capsule: half brown, half maroon), blood pressure stabilisers (another capsule, this one red and white), and fish oil (a jewel of a pill glittering in my palm). The most important of all is my anti-depressant, which can be broken in half along the imprinted line should I wish to take a smaller dose on a good day. I haven't had a good day yet.

Today isn't going to be a good one, either, judging by the blue intruder nestling in the carpet's pile under our bed, on David's side. I didn't realise what it was until I googled it.

It makes no sense. David and I *do* have sex It's just that it's usually over in a minute or two (no exaggeration), whereas with Viagra it's meant to go on for hours. Hours… No. It's beyond my ability to picture it.

David appears in the bedroom. "Mags? Are you okay?"

I hide the blue behind my iPhone. "Just lost the plot there, for a while," I reply. "Middle-age dementia."

He's supposed to draw me into his arms and tell me I'm forever young. That's the deal. He's five years my junior, and it's his job to tell me how it doesn't matter. But he only nods, as if remembering that I'm on the wrong side of forty-five. This enrages me more than the little blue pill.

As a lawyer, I know the dangers of accusing on the strength of circumstantial evidence. Before I condemn David, I need proof. Fortunately, the online computer shop has a local branch and employs a lovely young man who agrees to install webcams at our house while David is at the gym.

"One by the front door," I tell the young man. "One by the garden entrance. And one in the bedroom."

"Don't you want them to be visible? They usually work wonders as a deterrent to burglars."

"No."

The young man, he must be in his twenties, gives me a look. "If your husband's cheating on you," he says, "he's stupid as well as blind."

That puts me in high spirits until the next day, when I review the webcam footage and discover that the combination of a young busty brunette and a little blue pill can indeed last for hours.

I swallow an extra anti-depressant. I've never taken two of them in one day, but then, I've never before watched my husband star in a porn movie. So now what? We don't have children, David and I. His choice. It allows us to exist comfortably on my income, while he writes the next *Girl with the Dragon Tattoo*.

He's always been able to charm me stupid, so I can just imagine how easily he would talk me out of divorcing him. I can't think what else to do, so I go home.

"Mags," David says as soon as I walk in, "we need to rethink our insurance portfolio."

He means life insurance. For the rest of the evening his mouth is full of words like "the cash value of a permanent life insurance policy", "pulling from our benefits if we get really sick", "a guaranteed rate of return and zero downside exposure" and "protecting loved ones". As I don't have other family, that implies him.

He's so glib that I promise to collect the papers tomorrow, before my brain engages and starts wondering why now and what David is plotting.

"We can fill in the online application form right away," he says. His laptop is already on the right website. He takes his blue gaze off me to focus on the screen, and just like that, the hypnotic spell is broken, replaced by a jolt of fear.

The adrenaline rush puts me into an extra gear I never knew I possessed. My mind is as sharp as a sword, my senses on fire. I fake a big yawn. "Tomorrow," I tell him. "It's past midnight and I have an early start in the morning."

I wonder whether the life policy has an exclusion clause for suicide and how long you have to be a member before they pay out. I wonder how he's planning to get rid of me once I sign the insurance papers. Something that wouldn't arouse suspicion. And then I wonder whether I'm trying to discover how David is planning to kill me, or to plan his murder. A double dose of sleeping tablets helps me get a night's rest.

When I wake up in the morning, I know exactly how to do it. The pills for lowering my blood pressure will become my salvation in more ways than just one. The doctor is forever reminding me that I'm not allowed to adjust the dosage myself because an incorrect measure could lead to a stroke. Time to put that theory to the test.

I use a public library computer to look up the quantities. David's Sunday afternoon coffee contains just enough pressure pills. The ambulance people are very kind but not optimistic.

Andy, the young man from the webcam shop calls a few weeks later to follow up on the webcams. We meet up for coffee. There's a brief awkwardness as we deal with David's permanent residency in an assisted-living facility, then spend the rest of the time chatting about me. It's been years since anybody thought my corporate law work exciting.

"I've always wanted to be a lawyer," Andy says. "I

started the computer shop to earn the university fees, but the business never makes enough."

I consider his unspoken suggestion. The house is kind of empty without David. And Andy's young enough not to need Viagra for many, many years.

The Art of Old Age

New Zealand Herald, 21 June 2013

Robber raids elderly victims

Police are warning the elderly in Auckland to be wary after several were confronted by a robber – in some cases while he was lying in ambush awaiting their return home.

There have been eight incidents in recent days where people have been challenged and robbed while they were at home. In all cases the victims were elderly.

Sometimes I wonder who these people used to be, the ones I rob. They all look the same, dotted with freckles of old age, their skin leathered and thinned and in urgent need of ironing. Their shoulders are always caved in, their backs rounded like tortoise shells, and their eyes emit that switched-off look even when they stare right at you from above the gag.

Sometimes I wonder whether it's an ex-model I'm tying to her dining room chair, as rickety as her eighty-year-old frame. Or whether the old man who's pissed his pants in fear used to swish about – immortal and forever young – in his sports car.

Or whether this couple, holding hands as they shuffle hand-in-hand into their golden-years cottage where I lie in wait, used to bicker the way my parents did. Have they ever been unfaithful? Felt tempted to throttle the living daylights out of one another? Is the hand-in-hand shuffle a bluff? Usually I can tell as soon as they see me. It's whether they choose to protect themselves or the spouse.

50

The old Rimu floor looks like solid honey but it's hell on my elbows. Give me a carpet over wooden planks any day.

With single old folks, I knock on the door and pretend to sell vacuums or cheaper electricity plans. Sometimes I'm a gas inspector or a police officer. Starved for company and for something to do with their infinitely long day, they usually let me in.

Couples are trickier. That's why I wait for them inside.

Here they come now. The garden gate squeaks on its slanted hinges. I part the slats of the Venetian blind. The old woman has her thin arm zigzagged through his, the *Louis Vuitton* handbag hanging off the other arm for counterbalance. Against all odds, she's wearing high heels. Not stilettos, granted, but still about a metre too high for an old bird like her.

The old geezer is carrying a plastic bag from the local electronic shop. Oh, good. Normally, I take what is in their houses and wallets, which doesn't amount to a lot. A brand-new gadget, still in its box and with a receipt attached is a bonus.

Old age is a nuisance, I think.

My wife switches her bag to the other hand and weaves her arm through mine to steady herself.

Anybody who's experienced the aches, the insomnia, the shortness of breath, can tell you that old age sucks. For me, though, old age is more than a nuisance. It's a nightmare.

I used to run ten kilometres every morning to stay fit. My handgun would find its target within a hundred metres. I was a wizard with explosives. The perfect spheres of my biceps could lift a woman and throw her onto a bed. I used to do a fair amount of that back in Russia, before I met my wife. And after, if truth be told. What can I say? The times were tough, the future uncertain. Under Stalin and under those who came after him, we learnt to take life one day at a time, one pleasure at a time, one enemy at a time.

Back then, we knew the meaning of the word *fear*. Fear made me fake and kill friends and brown-nose my way out of trouble.

And now? Now I'm holding a new laptop computer a thousand times more powerful than Stalin ever was. Now my greatest problem is that the footpath between our garden gate and the front door is strewn with brown leaves, as ugly as the face I see in the mirror when shaving.

Old age is more than a nuisance and a nightmare. It's also unsightly.

My wife lets go of my arm, pokes the key into the lock and turns the handle. "Tea with jam?" she asks.

She used to offer blowjobs in that tempting tone. Now it's tea. Old age, I tell you, it's worse than death.

"Tea with jam?" I ask.

My husband has no time to reply. A shadow detaches itself from the window and pins him to the floor. Isn't it the other way around, I wonder, aren't you supposed to pin your shadow down? I'm sure there was a story like that.

I used to like stories, back when I was young. Younger. Back then, my husband was a great storyteller, able to explain every smear of lipstick on his collar, every bundle of hundred-rouble notes hidden under the mattress, every visit from grey-suited officials. I ooh-ed and aah-ed and nodded. Knew better than to believe a single word.

While my husband played soldier-spy, I tinker-tailored our existence from a room shared with two other couples into our own luxurious villa on the peripheries of Moscow and a palace-like dacha on the pebbly beach of the Black

Sea. I had the body and the brain to achieve it. I had the cunning and the KGB training to hold onto what I'd achieved, and once the system had crumbled, I had the foresight to flee to New Zealand.

While my husband is flailing on the beautiful wooden floor, in vain trying to force his muscles to remember how to be the James Bond of the Eastern Block, I swing my designer handbag. The weight of makeup, hand cream, hairbrush, coins for the parking meter, three pens, a book and everything else we women carry around, makes contact with the intruder's skull.

Before he has time to recover, I yank off one of my shoes and aim its heel at his temple. It's not my first time. It's why I always wear heels, even on days when my lower back is demanding slippers.

The beauty of old age is that nobody ever expects it to fight back.

"You get rid of the body," I tell my husband. "Like in the old days. Meanwhile, I'll make the tea."

I feel half a century younger. Perhaps we should do this again. Soon.

New Zealand Herald, 21 December 2013

Christmas for Cops

The last six months saw a sudden plunge of burglary statistics across Auckland. But the real Christmas gift for our police force came when they entered twenty-five abandoned premises, each full of stolen goods.

"It's like Christmas has come early," says Detective Ian Macdonald. "We got this anonymous letter with the addresses. Had no idea what we'd find."

The police are still looking for the owners or lapsed tenants of the properties, but word on the street is they're not looking too hard.

Masks for Every Occasion

- I -

The journalist from the far-flung idyll of New Zealand was the first victim.

"A burglary gone wrong," Captain de Vos said. "It's a shame it had to happen to a tourist, though. Speak to the hotel security and wrap it up. Wouldn't want to miss the kick-off."

His error was understandable given the nature of South Africa's crime statistics.

It never occurred to him to engage my services as a crime profiler, even though we work together every day and sleep together most nights. This would have put us in jail in Apartheid South Africa a mere two decades ago, for he is as white as an elephant tusk and I'm the black of the triangle in our flag. It gives me a thrill, as a law enforcement agent, to be doing something so akin to taboo.

That afternoon the country shut early. De Vos and I watched the broadcast of the FIFA World Cup opening match together. With all five of my brothers playing soccer, and one of them a reserve in this competition, I felt I was more than a spectator.

The atmosphere was brilliant. Hypnotised by the beehive hum of the vuvuzelas emitting from the TV and the calming rhythm of the game, I slipped into bliss. Even my headache had ebbed.

Thwack!

The first goal shook the entire stadium, eighty thousand throats exploding in primordial cries of triumph. My heart swelled like the Limpopo in the rainy season.

De Vos jumped off the sofa and punched the air freedom-fighter style.

"Yes!" He jerked me towards him and twirled us across the floor. "We may be ranked eighty-third, but we'll show them."

This was an interesting reaction from a man who wants to desert his land for the much greener grass of The Long White Cloud.

When we settled down, I snuggled into his embrace. "You know the journalist who was killed earlier today?"

"The Kiwi?" De Vos didn't move his eyes away from the screen. "It hasn't hit the news yet. They don't want it to spoil the moment. Why?"

"He was here to comment on the World Cup." I pulled my laptop towards us. "I'll show you the last article he wrote for his newspaper."

The tongue-in-cheek piece was titled, "Soccer Increasingly Boring Because Losing No Longer A Capital Offence".

"Ironic," said de Vos.

I liked his observation so much I included it in my personal blog that night. By morning, my entry had acquired an anonymous comment. *"Look for the offender's signature: it's more idiosyncratic than the modus operandi."*

- II -

17 June 2010

The sleaze-ball's face wore polite boredom like a tribal mask. I swallowed the urge to ram my ballpoint down his throat. Across the desk from me sat the man who'd raped at least three tourists at knifepoint as they were leaving Soccer City after late-night games. He was arrested thanks to my profiling. All I had to do was prove his guilt.

"Are you free for dinner tonight?" His vomit-inducing words drilled into my head. "We could watch the soccer. You're a fascinating woman, doctor…" He squinted at my nametag. "...Dr Elizabeth Mphela. I've never known a crime profiler before. What was your PhD on?"

I knew better than to answer, so I was surprised to hear my voice. "Multiple identity disorder."

"Oh yeah? Which of your identities wants to suck me off first?"

The pen felt slippery in my grip. *Do not strike him*, I heard inside me. *Do not strike.*

To calm down, I concentrated on my notes.

The suspect's aggressive stance and insistent denials indicate a reluctance to see himself as a sexual offender, making medical or psychiatric treatment unfeasible.

My phone pinged. I glanced at the subject line: "*New Murder Last Night, Drop Everything.*"

I tasted adrenaline on my tongue. "That will be all for today, Mr. Spencer. Thank you for your time. One of the detectives will escort you to your cell."

His grin showed too many teeth, too white and too sharp in his hairless skull shaped like a slug. "You know you don't have enough evidence to hold me. How about that soccer date?"

"I hope we'll meet again soon, Mr. Spencer, though definitely not for soccer."

For now, I read the email, concentrating on the pertinent facts. I recognised the victim's name, burned forever into the memory of all South Africans who had seen us lose thanks to his lack of refereeing skill.

Serves you right for red-carding our goalie last night, I thought.

When I got home that night, I blogged the sentiment. As the officials had put a clamp on all negative news during the Cup, I phrased it as a hypothetical question: "*Who's more at fault: a soccer player who dives or a ref who falls for it?*"

Lo and behold, the next morning, another anonymous comment was on my blog: "*The blame is equal. Victimology identifies similarities between each of the victims of a particular crime to establish a definite pattern.*"

Dread took its prickly constitutional down my spine. Whoever was responding to my blog was no layman.

It should have tipped me off. It probably would have. Only, I got a text message from my brother, the FIFA bench-warmer: "*I will be playing in the third match.*"

The red card turned out to be a blessing for one family, at least. That evening, our whole clan gathered to celebrate on home-brewed sorghum beer. It didn't contain battery acid like some of the *isikilimikwiki*[1], the kill-me-quickly some people make, nevertheless, I spent the whole of Saturday tending my head. Time stretched and shrank in unrealism like a Salvador Dali painting. I slept.

- III -

20 June 2010

The third victim's hotel suite belonged in a brothel, or at least in my idea of what a brothel should look like. A circular bed. A large mirror on the ceiling. Red plush chairs with gilded legs and armrests. An opened champagne bottle in an ice bucket of sludge.

"How long?" I asked.

"A few hours ago. Three tops. More likely under two."

I checked the time. The victim had played in the soccer match against New Zealand earlier that afternoon, finishing just before 6 pm. De Vos and I had watched it at the police station together, because one, I am a soccer addict and two, because de Vos loves all things New Zealand. Oh, how

---

[1] Moonshine, home-made alcohol

colourfully he swore when, in a time-warp replay of the South African match four days ago, an unjust penalty was awarded against the All Whites…

Victimology. My voice came out all hollow. "This guy. Is he the striker who did the dive against New Zealand?"

The medical examiner must have been the only person in the country not struck with World Cup fever. Or perhaps he simply didn't watch the match. Unlike de Vos, not all South Africans want to emigrate to New Zealand.

"Huh?" he replied. "This is a soccer player, Elizabeth, not a scuba diver."

I laughed despite myself. "Yeah, you're right there. I wish more soccer players realised it."

I took another look around me. It was a hotel suite in which soccer players entertain their groupies or underage prostitutes. Judging by the multi-shaded lipstick stains on the champagne glasses and on the victim's skin, this room was used for pretty much the same purpose. I counted the colours. Four. Despite myself, I felt something close to impressed. I know our Zulu boys can give a girl a good time many times in one evening, but I never imagined Europeans capable of the same feat.

I moved around swiftly, doing my job. Ostensibly, this looked like yet another burglary in which the perpetrators panic and take the crime to a higher level. It wasn't.

"The third crime scene looks identical to the previous two," I said into my *Blackberry*. Oh, the wonders of modern technology, when your phone is also your dictaphone and web browser. I'm waiting for the day this compilation of miracles comes out as a wristwatch with 3D output. "The victim was shot with a single bullet to the head. The modus operandi as well as the selection of victims seems to indicate a single killer."

Victimology. I had to figure out what the three victims had

in common, apart from soccer. A journalist, a ref, a striker. New Zealander, Swiss, Italian. The first victim may have offended any soccer fan. The second one was hated by all South Africa supporters, the third one by the Kiwis. It didn't add up.

"By the way," I asked as I packed up, "where are we with our soccer fan rapist?"

De Vos shook his head.

I could feel my nostrils dilate, my pulse hot against my eardrums. "You let him go?"

"We had nothing concrete. Condoms are a wonderful invention against AIDS, but they don't help cases such as these."

"Hair?" I asked desperately. Then, remembering his completely bald head, "Body hair?"

"The bastard shaves everything."

"Fuck."

The media was told nothing and all the personnel working on the case received a stern warning not to talk to anybody outside our circle, so my blog entry consisted of a row of question marks.

That didn't stop my anonymous comment-writer. Before long, the following words appeared in the comments box: *"Every serial killer works to a certain set of self-imposed values, values as unique and identifiable as handwriting."*

I couldn't have put it better myself.

Trouble was, what fucking values?

Justice, whispered something inside my mind.

I ignored it.

- IV -

26 June 2010

It all went conspiracy-story after that. The official story, supported by the striker's coach, was that the player got food poisoning and would not play in the last match of the pool stage. I wondered what excuse they would concoct if his team did make it to the eliminations, but that wasn't to be.

South Africa also fell out, despite my brother's dazzling play in the last match of the group stage. While the rest of the country swayed under the blow, I secretly harboured the hope this would herald the end of the serial killings.

Nobody else shared my hope. The direct elimination matches were about to commence and the boss was pushing me to predict the serial killer's next move.

"I need a result, Elizabeth," he said at the special team meeting this morning, his voice all no-nonsense and no-excuses.

I may be sleeping with de Vos, he may be hoping to persuade me to move to New Zealand with him, but he's still the boss when we're at work.

"Yes, Captain," was the only appropriate reply, though I did promise myself I'd get him back at home.

"Can you narrow the field for us?" he asked. "Race, age, geographical location?"

I shrugged. "Clearly someone who won't raise suspicions entering posh hotels. A local or at least a local for the duration of the World Cup, perhaps even a resident of one of the hotels. Someone smart enough to lay false clues like the burglaries. A soccer spectator or a soccer professional. Someone whom the victims were comfortable to entertain in their hotel rooms." You didn't have to be a crime profiler to come up with any of that. "Comfortable using a gun." Well, that narrowed it down. Not. Most South Africans, children and old people included, could shoot a gun in their sleep. "The gun is untraceable, I take it?"

De Vos nodded, stretched, got up. "Okay, people. We have a job to do."

It was a Saturday, but nobody was in a hurry to go home after the meeting. Back in my office, I stared at the wall. The desert-empty whiteboard hung like an accusation next to an A1 sheet with the schedule of all the World Cup matches. With a red marker, I recorded the names of the three victims, the dates of their deaths, their professions. I didn't need to do this, good memory is in every African's genes, but I felt better for having done something.

Next, in green and thankfully very much "delible" ink, I composed a list of suspects.

- Disgruntled soccer fan.
- Disgruntled player.
- A gambler trying to improve the odds for his wager.
- Somebody who wanted to kill only one of the victims and used the others as a smokescreen.
- A fellow crime profiler.

Point number five chafed me and I rubbed it out with the heel of my hand. Yet it was hard to argue with the facts. Back it went. No, anybody could walk in and see it.

In the end, I settled for an acronym, FCP, Fellow Crime Profiler. Great. Now what?

Made fashionable among the general public by Hollywood, criminal profiling is the grey area between law enforcement science and the art of psychology. It's a relatively new field with no set methodology and few guidelines for the practitioners. I spent the rest of the day following bullet trajectories and running statistical analysis on anything that could be analysed.

"Coming to watch the game?" de Vos stood in the doorway, a six-pack balanced in the palm of his hand, which was so huge it dwarfed the cans.

I shrugged. "Dunno. Who's playing? Uruguay and…?" I couldn't remember.

Funny that. When South Africa fell out of the competition, it had taken some of my soccer spirit with it. I still liked the sport, but suddenly it was not a matter of patriotism to watch it. I would do my country a far greater service if I could catch the serial killer.

"Who cares who else," snapped de Vos. "We want to see Uruguay lose."

He had a point. The great Diving Divas of Italy had already gone home. It was time to send the Uruguayan Scuba Team packing.

"Come on, Elizabeth, please. It's Saturday. Your place, my beer?"

I capitulated. "Whatever you say. You're the boss."

Two hours later, the boss changed into a thoroughbred soccer fan.

"What a swine," de Vos raged. The beer can crunched, crushed by his fist. Beer dregs ran down his elbow onto the lounge carpet. Mine. "Did you see that? Elizabeth, did you see? What a diver. What a performer. What a fake."

"Mmmmm." There is something hypnotic and mesmerising in soccer's rhythm. I was in my zone, reluctant to surface.

De Vos had found his groove. "Doesn't he know this is South Africa? It's a dangerous country in which to get on the wrong side of the crowd."

I said nothing.

"Elizabeth."

"What? The ref isn't buying any of it. Just sit down, relax, enjoy the game."

He got all huffy with me and left as soon as the game was over, ranting at Uruguay's victory.

I felt another massive headache coming on, so I went straight to bed. Before I fell asleep, I blogged a few disjointed lines on the topic of *"It's the coach's fault anyway for letting them fake injuries"*.

I was jerked awake by a phone call from de Vos. "We have another one."

My head still hurt. Even before he said it, though, I knew. I let him say it anyway. "The Uruguayan coach."

"I'll be right there. Which hotel?"

Despite my promise, I didn't leave straight away. The laptop took forever to boot up and to find a signal. The ISP dropped out three times before I got to my blog page.

The anonymous comment, left three hours earlier, read: *"According to Turvey, behavioural analysis, with its "magical" quality, is not effective in practice. Not only do criminals think differently than most people, but their behaviour has different meanings in different cultures."*

There was no escaping it. The perp knew about Brent Turvey, an expert in forensic science. He was one of us.

- V -

6 July 2010

Bribery is most resplendent on the elephant hide of Africa's soil. Despite the international flavour of the murders, the facts slipped away unnoticed by the media.

A voice in my head said it was a good thing. My boss said I had a job to do. I listened to both.

Predominantly, serial killers come from dysfunctional families. They are almost always assumed to be men, and that's true when the murders go hand in hand with sexual assault on the victim. Black Widows and Angels of Death, though, are predominantly women. While male serial killers kill for sexual reasons, female ones typically kill for profit.

The FIFA murders didn't fit the bill.

Perhaps what I needed was the German octopus, the one that predicted the results of all the German matches. Or perhaps, now that crime profiling methods proved useless, I could resort to some good old-fashioned sleuthing.

"Has anybody reviewed any of the hotels' security tapes?" I asked de Vos.

He shot me a meerkat-caught-in-the-headlights look. "Er… We reviewed a lot of soccer footage?"

The way he said it made me laugh, and I nuzzled his chest before I appropriated his computer and settled for a day of boredom. Given the choice between watching security tapes and watching paint dry, I'd always go for the latter. Watching paint dry is at least less taxing on the eyes.

De Vos had already done all the grunge work of selecting the recordings taken around the times of the murders, so I was spared having to fast forward through hours of irrelevant copy.

I recognised the leather jacket on the footage of the first murder, but it took me two more to realise what I was seeing. Every time, the leather jacket had arrived at the hotel *before* the body was discovered.

This was not happening. A round hard ball of foreboding lodged in my throat. Slowly, every shift forward an effort, I walked towards the closet where we kept our coats in winter, when the African mornings are cold enough to freeze water in the pipes.

The mossy green of the leather peeked from behind my red woollen poncho and de Vos's duffle coat with big rectangular buttons. Inside the right-hand pocket, my hand encountered the familiar shape of metal death.

No hesitation, no second thoughts, no guilty conscience. I began by hard-erasing the footage from de Vos's computer. Nobody was likely to miss it for the moment, and I made a mental note to return with a powerful magnet to complete the job. Task one, check.

Task two. "Captain?" I said in my best professional voice. "Would a specialist be able to trace an anonymous comment placed on a blog?"

"Theoretically. You need the blog owner's permission, or you have to serve a court order on their ISP provider to get the data. Why? Do we have something?"

The anticipation in his voice was almost heartbreaking. Almost.

"No, sorry. It was just a random thought. I wanted to give hell to the FIFA officials for not coming down harder on all the cheating. Where is the sportsmanship in soccer? The cheaters actually gloat about it afterwards." Task three, delete those comments. Make that, delete the whole blog.

"Your brother played first-class soccer, though," de Vos said, his hand briefly on my shoulder. "He'll show them the true meaning of the game in Brazil."

I nodded. The next World Cup seemed light years away.

Now for task four. I'm not proud of what I did next. Yet I did it, I, Elizabeth Mphela, PhD. I take full responsibility.

Funny thing, though, human conscience. Mine didn't bother me one bit as I pleaded a headache to de Vos and told him to watch the soccer without me.

I arrived at my destination just before the semi-final kick-off. Neither match was held at Soccer City, so I was sure he'd be home.

"Hi, Mr. Spencer," I said to the camera at his gate. Task five, destroy this footage when I'm done. "I've come to take you up on your dinner invitation."

The fool let me in.

It was child's play to shoot him with the same gun as the one used by the serial killer. Live by the sword, die by the sword. No remorse. Thanks to my training, I knew exactly where to place it to make it look like suicide.

I used his computer to send a confession to the general police email address I found on the web. Then I watched the game on his television. Uruguay lost the semi-final. Justice prevailed.

It was me, my own identity, all the time. No headache, no time warp, no memory loss.

What I'd loved most about my doctoral thesis was the controversy surrounding the existence of the multiple identity disorder. Now I loved the irony.

My Blackberry rang. I checked the caller ID. De Vos, the man with only one identity.

"How's your head?"

"Good."

"Will you marry me?"

I thought about it. "Will you make me move to New Zealand?"

"Probably. Is that a problem? The All Whites are good."

I thought some more. "Okay."

It was more than okay. New Zealand. What were the chances of a tiny nation like theirs hosting a World Cup?

First published in *Guilty Consciences* Anthology, UK, November 2011

The Connoisseur

My brain goes fuzzy. Can't decide what to order. They don't have lobster, or duck, or snails. (Not that I think snails are the pinnacle of gourmet. Unless the chef really knows what he's doing, snails often come out rubbery and greasy with garlic butter.)

I don't trust them to prepare an authentic Thai banana curry, or to marinade the chicken properly for a tandoori dish.

They tell me to make up my mind. Could do me a nice steak, they say. Trouble is, I don't want nice. I want exquisite. I want taste to die for. I want to remember this meal for the rest of my life.

They assure me I will.

And they tell me to hurry the f-ck up or they'll just get me fish fingers and chips for my last meal request.

Doesn't sound too bad, to be honest. I remember the softness of homemade potato chips my mother used to cook every Friday night. The salt would burn my mouth and the vinegar would grate my throat with its sour fingers. The fish was crumbly and bland by comparison, a poultice after the stinging chips. And for dessert… my imagination can taste the thick custard, the juicy currants, the innocence of childhood.

After a life of caviar and *Brut* champagne, I know the exact combination of flavours and textures that will be my final meal.

"I want spotted dick," I tell them.

They are still laughing as they slam the cell door shut.

Their voices reverberate in the tomblike silence. "Dead Man Eating."

Dear Future Me

Dear Future Me,

If you're reading this, it's because the worst case scenario has happened and you've lost all your memory. Well, not all of it. You still remember how to get dressed, and to breathe in and out approximately sixty times every minute.

Your name is Amy Cooper and you're thirty-nine years old. You used to fret about turning forty, but now you're beginning to realise there are worse things in life than getting older.

Like not remembering your children, for example. You have three wonderful children. Kyle is fifteen and pretty amazing for a teenager: no sulking, no backchat, no sign of drugs or drinking. The middle daughter, Anastasia, is twelve, loves netball and hates her name being abbreviated to Ana. Florence is only six and I worry about her the most – will she still remember the real me? Or will the word mother be forever linked in her brain to an empty shell of a woman sitting in the armchair without a thought in her head?

The doctors don't know what's wrong with you. Amnesia, yes, that's easy to diagnose, but they can't tell whether it's an early onset of Alzheimer's or whether you've had a mini-stroke. They've done a lot of tests – inconclusive – and said the memory would either slowly improve or get worse, that'll be seven hundred dollars, thank you very much. Must be cool to be a doctor, huh? So, seeing as you're reading this, my bet is on the latter option.

Some quick trivia about you. You like the colour blue: cornflower blue, not navy. Your favourite book is an obscure one by Joshilyn Jackson about maternal love. As a child, you used to love chocolate, the brown in-between kind, not the dark or the white kind, but lately sugar tastes like poison to you, so if you have dessert now, it's usually fruit or cheese.

You love your family more than anything in the world. Your husband was your first love, childhood sweethearts and all the clichés that go with it. I can't imagine I need to remind you, feelings probably won't disappear together with the memory, but just in case.

Am a bit worn out at the moment, not to mention weepy, so I'll write more later. I'll hide this in my knitting basket. Nobody else ever opens it.

Until next time,
Me

Dear Future Me,

You married a good man. He's not perfect – who is – but there's a good heart beating inside his chest. It's a nice chest, by the way, have you seen it yet? One fine thing about losing your memory – and I'm scraping the bottom of the barrel here – is that your sex life is bound to be amazing. All the grudges and bad associations will be gone with your memory, and you'll be able to enjoy the forty-two year old stranger who's sharing your bed.

I'll leave it to you to discover all his faults, so here are a few of the many positives: he's solid like the ground you walk on, hardworking, reliable. If that sounds a tad boring, rest assured, it's not. The fence gets mended the same week it falls over, moss never gets a chance to grow on the driveway, and extra hooks appear in the pantry as if by magic, before you open your mouth to ask for them.

Be kind to him. If our daughters marry somebody like Brett one day, they'll be lucky. Sometimes I wonder what type of man they're going to choose, given that Anastasia's role model for true love is based on Twilight: a creepy cold guy who steals into the bedroom to watch his sweetheart sleep. With vampires like Edward What's-His-Face and business tycoon bullies like Christian Grey, it looks like Prince Charming is truly dead for this generation of growing-up girls.

Not to say Brett is Prince Charming. He is one better. He may never bring you roses, but he'll love you with love that is steadfast and from the bottom of his soul.

Brett's favourite food is roast lamb, no mint, with garlic potato wedges and green beans. The whole family adores it. You're lucky Brett makes enough money for you to be a stay-at-home mum. I was going to lie and say you love cooking, but nah, you'd cotton on sooner or later. The truth is you enjoy thinking up new food, yet the family – Kyle in particular – is strangely adverse to pork chops in chocolate sauce and strawberries in mustard, so you end up cooking same-old, same-old, which drives you nuts. At least baking cookies with Florence is a treat, and Anastasia can make apple crumble and lamb stew all by herself.

Which reminds me. Best start on the dinner.

Until next time,

Me

Dear Future Me,

Do you believe human beings have souls? You must, because I do. I'm sitting in the garden, drinking my first cup of Earl Grey and flicking through my wedding album. The sun is warm on my back, my ears are filled with the sweet whistles of the tui[2], and the cogs in my mind are turning, churning, whirring.

If I lose my memory, where will my soul go? Whose soul will you have? Will we share? And in the afterlife, provided there is an afterlife, will you be responsible for my sins and I for yours? Will we meet and recognise each other, or will we co-exist without being aware of the other's existence?

Who will be married to my Brett?

That's what I'm thinking about as I drink my tea. Milk, no sugar. Is that how you take yours?

Musingly,
Me

Hi Me

Today you are more real than usual, and to say I'm not happy would be the understatement of the century. After a lengthy visit and even more tests, the specialist pronounced my progress as negative. Soon I'll start repeating myself, soon I'll forget what I had for breakfast, soon I'll have trouble finding words to express even the simplest concepts. That last prediction scared me somewhat, because I enjoy words.

Right now, though, I don't feel like writing. Must be that water in my eyes. Or maybe it's that tight feeling in my chest, as though I've swallowed an unpeeled pineapple.

Me

---

[2] A boisterous songbird native to New Zealand

Dear Future Me,

It was my fortieth birthday today. No matter what the doctors say, this day I'll remember forever.

Brett pulled out all the stops. The day started with breakfast in bed and a trip to a spa, where I had an orange-scented bath, a facial and a full-body massage. Bliss! Lunch was a picnic at the beach – the weather played along and the basket was full of goodies the kids made at home. That's where I got my present, too, a gold locket with a photo of all five of us. I think they meant it for when I lose my memory, and a sharp shard of dread lodged itself in my heart, but it melted away almost instantly. My family and this day, two things I'll never forget.

When we finally got home, I opened the front door to shouts of "surprise!" And surprised I was. Brett hates parties, and organising is not his thing, so I knew it was a biggie for him. Helium balloons, champagne and a cake done without sugar – just for me. He remembered I don't eat sweets anymore.

You are one lucky woman, Future Me.

Me (now forty years old)

Dear Future Me

Forty doesn't feel any different to thirty-nine. Last night, I asked Brett what it was like to be married to a forty-year old. Apparently, it's awesome. Told you he's a keeper.

I can't believe the time will come when I won't even remember he'd said that. I can't believe I'll forget I dislike cigarette smoke. I can't believe I'm losing my past.

To think other forty-year olds worry about their boobs sagging. In a few months' time, I won't remember what mine looked like before anyway.

Me

Dear Future Me

Yesterday I got angry with you, the Future Me waiting to replace me. You want my life? I wanted to shout. Sure! Here is my apron, my boots and my makeup box. Here's the children's after-school schedule, remember Anastasia has to be at the netball courts at least fifteen minutes before the match. The dog needs to be walked at least once a day and he throws up supermarket pet food. Have it all.

I'm so afraid of not existing anymore. There's a Keats poem about it, When I Have Fears That I Cease To Be. Look it up sometime.

I keep telling myself it could be worse. It's not like I'm dying. Even when my memories are gone, I'll still be here for the kids. Or you will be, at any rate. They might laugh when you can't remember what seven times eight is, but at least they'll still have you to love and to cuddle and to make Brett his favourite meal. It's roast lamb, by the way, have I told you that already? Can't remember.

I want them to know how much I love them. You will tell them for me, won't you? Every day.

Me

Dear Future Me

If you're reading this, it's because the worst has happened and you've lost your memory. So here's a quick summary of things you need to know.

Your name is Amy Cooper and you are thirty-nine

years old. You're a bit unhappy about the big four-oh looming, but you're looking forward to your birthday party. You're hoping it'll be something unforgettable, something to hold on to, even when all other memories evaporate from your brain.

The doctors don't know what's wrong with you. They mention long medical words, most of them starting with the letter A.

The most important thing is you have three wonderful children: Kyle, Anastasia and Florence. You're married to a wonderful man, Brett. He likes lamb. I'll write more about them when this headache stops.

Meanwhile, I'll hide this in my... that wicker thing with wool inside.

Until next time,

Me

First published in *RWNZ Liaisons*, September 2014

Where Art Has No Place

Dedicated to those affected by the 2011 earthquake in Christchurch, New Zealand.

I've come to this city to forget. And, if truth be told, to change the world. But mostly to forget.

Changing the world is the easy bit. I spend my days painting the pavements of Christchurch the colours of spring and sunsets, I transform it into sea foam and mountains, I sketch portraits of passers-by the way they want to look.

I spend my nights chewing the bed sheets. Forgetting... I suck at forgetting. Even the guy with the dark blue eyes and the jawline as smooth as the first stroke of paint, the one who lives in the penthouse three floors above me, and whose smile warms up the elevator, fails to offer oblivion.

"Good afternoon," he says as soon as I step in. "Back from your lunch break already?"

"Er…" I hesitate. *Who cares what he thinks of me?* I opt for the truth. "Nah. I only just got up. Artist's privilege."

The elevator door slides closed, and I hold my breath, wishing the metal cage to descend. Logically, I understand it's programmed to obey the buttons and complete its journey all the way to the ground floor, yet I have this irrational fear it'll suddenly lurch upwards into the big unknown.

I live on the twelfth floor, its number labelled in Roman fashion with a decisive X followed by two rods. No reason it should feel any different from floor thirteen, which has only one more rod than mine, yet the other floors are alien and intimidating.

The elevator sinks and I exhale relief.

The penthouse guy watches my face. "Good morning

then. I wondered why I didn't see any new paintings when I got back from my morning meeting."

The penthouse guy does something terribly important in the computer industry. His offices are a block away, but he often works from home. *Not that I'm keeping tabs or anything.*

"You looked?" I can't keep the amateurish astonishment from my voice. *Grow some backbone, Vi*, I admonish myself. *You're a professional artist. You expect people to look.*

The blunder heats up my face all the way to where the neckline of my dress stops and then some.

His expression is serious with a few fault lines of laughter deepening in his left cheek. "I looked."

It's an old elevator and it takes its sweet time to reach the ground. Normally, the coward in me is grateful, but today I wish it to plunge down, unfettered.

"The canvases are five hundred dollars, if you're interested." Professional backbone. Why does it feel so out of place in this two-by-two metre enclosure filled with the spicy scent of his aftershave?

"I'm interested."

The low timbre of his voice reverberates inside my chest, beats inside my heart, clogs up my throat. *I'm interested. I'm interested. Interested.*

The elevator stops with a thud. I escape while the door is still opening, run away from the words, the aftershave, the eyes that are too blue for my own good.

The sidewalk is drenched in colour from yesterday's painting session. The chalk is smeared on the edges, where a careless foot touched it, but the overall effect still hits me between the eyes. It's good, I know it's good, and it'll look even better immortalised on canvas.

I open the padlock of the little storage room where I

keep my brushes and palettes and turps for the oil paints and water for the acrylic. Finished canvases line the short walls.

"Wow."

He followed me! My heart executes a dull thud in my throat for a beat before returning to its usual place.

"The larger-than-life colours make me think of journeying into outer space."

"I don't think there's much colour in outer space," I say. So much for professionalism. Rule number one: never disagree with a viewer's subjective experience of your work.

"Good point." He's still staring at the canvas. "Perhaps it's the depth. The shape of the coils."

Okay, I've worked it out. He's hitting on me.

"You don't have to say nice things about my paintings. Just ask me out for a drink."

"What?"

Oh no. He isn't hitting on me. I wish the earth could open up and swallow me whole.

It does.

Everything comes at once: the jolt, the booming noise, the sound of glass shattering.

"Just another aftershock," I say. I can't hear my own words. And it isn't just another aftershock. The courtyard splits open and my feet slide out from under me.

"I've got you."

A grip like a steel ring bites into my armpits and I'm flying upwards and onto the still vibrating concrete.

"Let's get out of here."

I agree. Everything in me screams for me to run. Trouble is, I can't move. *So this is what it feels like* echoes somewhere in the deepest recesses of my brain. *This is what a real earthquake feels like.*

"Get up. Now. It's not safe."

My legs are not obeying me.

"Victoria?"

It's all as surreal as the most daring painting I've ever created. The apartment building shudders. I wonder how he knows my name even as I watch a brick detach and sail towards us. My mouth opens. The brick makes contact with his head. I scream.

The sound is swallowed up by a sea of other screams. I'm alone. No matter. I can do this alone. History will not repeat itself.

I hurt all over, but my body works. He's still unconscious. I know I'm not supposed to move him. First aid must have been written by somebody who had never experienced an emergency. Regardless of concussion, we can't stay here.

One of my canvases is large enough to make a ground sheet. I roll the penthouse guy onto it and pull it like a sled onto the street. He groans but doesn't wake up. Someone spots us and says something.

I follow the crowd.

Much later, he opens his eyes and I'm grateful for first aid. "What's your name?" I ask. Standard textbook practice.

"Claude Monet."

"Oh." The gasp escapes before I realise he's smiling. "You jerk! Scared me stiff."

"Just checking."

"Checking?" I repeat.

"Whether you care."

"Oh." *A great comeback there, Vi. Try harder.* "And I'm Pablo Picasso," I say. "Pleased to meet you."

"Don't sell yourself short, girl. You're much better than Picasso."

I bite down hard to stop the third "oh" from escaping my lips. "I bet you say that to all the girls."

"Yep." He tries to nod, winces. "Standard pick-up line." His throat moves in a silent swallow. His lips are dry, caked with dust. "Say, about that drink you mentioned earlier…"

I'm grateful for the bottle of water I grabbed from my paint shed. The shelter is low on water.

At least the evening is high on stars. The sky is studded with them, Nature's way of compensating for the disaster.

"It's because there's no electricity," Troy says. Troy Holloway is the penthouse guy's real name. Though Claude would have been neat, too.

"No electricity," I repeat, disappointed. So much for Nature's compensation.

Troy's fingers find mine in the dark, squeeze snugly into the spaces in-between. "I know it's hard for you, Vi."

"It's hard for everybody."

"I know about…" He pauses briefly. "About Haiti. Your boyfriend was a hero."

My boyfriend. The one I try to forget. One of the charity volunteers who died in last year's earthquake.

"Ex-boyfriend," I correct gently. The guilt has choked me for thirteen months. "We split up before he went." I force the next bit out syllable by syllable. "That's why he went."

Troy's fingers keep an even grip on mine. "Makes it even harder."

I cry. Not for the first time, but as my sobs blend in with the many sobs of the survivors, I wonder whether it's the last time. There's so much misery around me, it would be a sin to live in the past.

We sleep together that night, Troy and I, sharing the canvas that used to be his stretcher. There should be nothing romantic about sleeping together in a hall full of strangers, and yet, in this hellhole, his arm touching mine all the way from shoulder to fingers is more intimate than a lovers' embrace.

The next morning, I try to capture the sky full of stars on the sidewalk outside the shelter. My medium is a piece of charred wood and a chalky brick.

A passer-by says, "You're wasting your time."

I just stare at her.

"Nobody wants art at a time like this. The city needs water. Toilets. Why not be useful? Take a shovel and dig a latrine."

Perhaps she is right. What good would my pictures do when the world folds up around us? What good did my pictures ever do? I should have studied medicine, like my parents told me to, not squander my brainpower on painting. If I were a doctor, or even a nurse, I'd be able to help this haemorrhaging city.

"She's wrong, you know." Troy's jaw, untouched by a razor, looks even harder than usual. "People need art at a time like this. They need beauty. Escapism."

"Escapism?"

Troy gestures towards the crumbled buildings, the dust that wouldn't settle, the uneven surface of the sidewalk trembling in yet another aftershock. "Many are talking about leaving the city for good."

Leave the city? The idea lodges in my soul like a shard of glass. Twenty-four hours ago this man meant nothing to me. Now I can't imagine life without him. "And you?"

He shakes his head. "I'm not going anywhere. Broken can still be beautiful."

I know he doesn't mean the city. Not only the city.

No Woman Is an Island

Laura's throat feels dry as ground pepper. She has never rowed before. Her arms ache. One-two. One-two.

Hopeless. Totally hopeless.

Robert's face flashes before her eyes. She wipes off the image together with the salt of her sweat and tears, loses the rhythm.

It's his fault she's rowing for her life. Him and that redhead from Marketing.

One-two. One-two. How much longer? She's getting nowhere. Here, in the rowing boat, as well as in her marriage. Their relationship crumbled after the twins came along.

But she'll show him.

The twins are better off this way.

She'll make him sorry.

The bell chimes. Laura climbs off the rowing machine. Inspects her newly sculpted body.

"Looking bloody awesome." her personal trainer stretches up both thumbs.

At that very moment, Laura snaps a selfie and posts it on her Instagram, muscles and personal trainer and all, where Robert is sure to look for updates on the twins.

She'll never take him back.

It's fun to make him wonder.

A Network Goddess

The drop-dead sexy interviewer makes it difficult for me to concentrate.

"Do you mind taking the night shift?" he asks. His mouth moves in a way that should be X-rated.

"Not at all." Relief relaxes my guard. "I prefer working nights." Means I can spend time with the kids during the day.

He raises his eyebrows in a silent question. The redhead from Human Resources, however, is already shaking her head, smiling an apology. "Unfortunately, we require our staff to be available all hours."

Damn. I want this job. Desperately. Will juggle plates while balancing on a ball to get it. "Naturally, I'm available whenever…"

The boss cuts in. "Welcome to the network administration team. I'm Josh."

"Tiffany." I extend my hand.

His handshake is solid and warm. Our first physical contact.

I see it all: what time you log in, whom you contact online, what sites you visit at midnight. I read your emails. I can pretend to be you. Change your status on *Facebook*. Trash your reputation.

I'm your network's admin. In a world controlled by computers, I'm a goddess.

For the first two weeks on the job, I behave. No straying into people's secrets in case I'm watched. Who watches the administrator? Her boss. And who watches Josh? I do.

I watch the way his jeans wrap around his hips. I watch his fingers caressing the keyboard. I watch…

"Tiffany?"

Whenever he says my name, I imagine it in his mouth, draped around his tongue, tickling his lips. I swallow my thoughts. "Yeah?"

"New virus."

I rush over. "Isolate it. Block the root. Quick!"

We huddle over his screen, work together like a pair of surgeons, communicating in monosyllables. So close I smell his citrus aftershave.

"Got it." Josh stretches, checks his watch. "Eggs on bagel to celebrate?"

I check my watch, too. Wince. "Sorry. Have to go home."

"Come on." He reminds me of the Big Bad Wolf tempting Red Riding Hood to step off the path. I want to taste his grin. Man, I have it bad.

Josh is young. Granted, I hardly look my thirty-two years, but I'd bet money Josh isn't a minute over twenty-eight. Not my type at all. I like my men older, seasoned with experience, mature enough to deal with the... complexity of my world.

And yet, and yet... Those eyes. Those tight jeans. Something tugs inside me, intense and unrelenting.

"How about a midnight snack tomorrow?"

"Cool."

His smile makes me forget my name.

The next evening, I gather the courage to break into his email account. No, *break into* is not accurate, *walk into* is more like it. As the network administrator, I have access to everything, like an omnipotent goddess. I have a table of user names and passwords, but I don't need it for this specific task. Though, I confess, I'm planning to use it someday soon.

I'm disappointed. Josh's emails are bland to the point

of blehhh. How can a hunk like him have such a boring inbox? Messages from his boss about the company's vision and mission, messages from Human Resources about staff issues (one is about me), complaints about Melissa who uses too much perfume and Mark who doesn't use enough. I go through his deleted folder. Not a single email from a friend, not a single forwarded joke. All his newsletters are IT-related. If this is the extent of Josh's cyber presence, he is either not real or hiding something wicked.

The email about me from Human Resources wants a progress report. The redhead expresses her concerns about my not integrating. I hate her, even as I read Josh's reply: "Tiffany is a delightful addition to our team, diligent, reliable and with tremendous integrity."

That last term bugs me. Integrity. I shrug. Integrity's overrated in my world.

"Tiffany," his voice anchors me back at work. "Somebody's trying to hack in."

I sort it in five minutes. Spend the rest of the time on Josh.

This is when I use the table of users and passwords. Amazing what you can discover about people by analysing their passwords. Some use a variant of their own name – The Narcissists, I call them. Others settle on the name of their loved one – they are The Boring Bunch. Some think they're clever to substitute numbers for letters, like 1L0VEs3x.

Josh's network password makes me gasp. TIFFANY. I check how old it is. The date sends a handful of ice down my spine. Josh changed the password an hour after he'd hired me.

A clear message. A warning to cease prying? Or an invitation into his online world?

Most people use the same password for everything: email,

screensaver, bank account. Josh's TIFFANY password, however, doesn't work on any of his other sites. I can't get into his *Facebook*, or *eBay*, or… hang on, an e-book store lets me log in.

I look through the titles he's purchased of late, every single one punching a hole through my chest.

- Creating a Happy Blended Family
- Making It As a Stepdad
- 10 Steps to Conquer Steptrouble

Damn and blast.

He knows.

And he wants me to know he knows.

I call off the midnight snack. Need to think. Am I ready to trust him with my children? Or should I clear out, move cities, the way I always do? My stepfather was one mean bastard. He taught me to lie, to steal and to never wish a step-parent on anybody, especially not on my own children.

Okay. Run it is. For that, I need money. A good thing I'm the network goddess. The table of passwords tells me the redhead from Human Resources is a Narcissist who uses GinaWork as her password. Her browsing history reveals which bank she uses. I guess her bank password to be GinaBank. Bingo! Suck all the funds out of her account, gush them into a money-laundering company, transfer into my own Swiss bank. Done. Easy when you know how.

As I'm waiting for my shift to end, an *Insufficient Funds* message pops into Josh's inbox. Why into Josh's? Quickly, before he spots the email, I forward it into my personal mail folder. My hands quiver as I click-open the note.

It's about insufficient funds in Gina's account to make the automatic withdrawal of $5. But why alert Josh about it? I read the email again, think, trawl through the automatic software running on our network.

One of the apps is programmed to extract five dollars a

night from every employee's bank account, without making a record of the transaction, and to place it in a financial institution in the Azores. Every employee, including me. The impertinence of it! I run a hack, but the Azores security is as solid as that of my own Swiss bank. Tracking down the author of the app, though, is a no-brainer: after all, the warning went into *his* inbox.

Josh. A thief, like me, abusing his god-like powers of network administration. Wow. Suddenly he's more than a hot guy. He is competition. Yet my pulse quickens. I hear the rapid rush of blood to my head. Bad boys – who can resist them?

"Tiffany?"

I look up. Think of the devil… Josh's standing in front of his computer. All I see is his back, but I sense the tension in his shoulders.

"I saw what you did to Gina's account," he says.

Run, a voice screams inside my head.

Josh turns around and looks straight at me. "That was… brazen. Brilliant. Sexy."

I don't move. We're two of a kind, attracted to the dark. An unexpected jolt of happiness bolts through my body, sending a rebellious strand of hair falling across my cheek. Josh sweeps it off gently, joining it with the rest of my curls, running his fingers through them, stroking, tugging. Not sexual and yet arousing, calming and thrilling at once. I'm hungry for his hands, for his skin, for his words that set my world on fire.

"Come on." His voice trickles out thick. "You know you want to."

An understatement.

No relationships, the voice inside me cautions.

His fingers leave my hair and seep their warmth into my neck. "We're going to be so good together."

Yeah.

Perhaps we could… just this once?

Run!

The anticipation builds up inside me, scorching and tight. Whoever said the waiting was the best part couldn't have been more wrong. It takes all my willpower to postpone the gratification. I count the minutes, my imagination full of Josh. Josh in my apartment, in my bed…

Sex leads to love, the silly voice pipes up again.

Oh, shut up.

"No strings," I say out loud.

Josh nods, his expression comically solemn. "None."

"No living together."

He hesitates. When he speaks, his voice is raw with honesty. "Sorry if my step-parenting books gave you the creeps. I'm not looking for an instant family. But if the woman of my dreams arrives on my doorstep, I sure as hell won't shy away from her baggage."

That's probably the most romantic thing I've ever heard. I search for something equally atmospheric to reciprocate. "Eggs on bagel after sex?" I ask.

Never said I was the goddess of smooth talking.

Superheroes of Yesteryear

As soon as I realise it's my granddaughter sitting there, I know we're in trouble. My mind lists the alternatives, all of them feasible, all of them disturbing: a bomb planted in Heathrow's Business Class Lounge; an aeroplane crash; terrorists taking over the airport, like in one of the *Die Hard* movies. I check my mobile phone. No alerts. Odd. My employers should be onto whatever situation is brewing.

Next, I try to catch my granddaughter's eye, and fail so dismally, she must be doing it on purpose. Her attention is focused on an elderly – ahem – on a gentleman in the prime of his years. There's something familiar in the tilt of his head, even though the silver hair is all wrong: it should be the brown of milk chocolate. The shoulders, still as straight as they were half a century ago, should be broader.

Can't be. But as soon as he looks up, I know it is. The blue of his eyes not faded with time, his gaze when it catches mine is as intense as ever. Matt.

My throat closes around the sudden intake of breath. There's a vacuum in my ears and a thudding in my chest. Matt, my best friend from the sandpit. Throughout childhood and adolescence, we were so used to saying we were "just friends" and that we didn't "like one another in that way", I guess we just never stopped to regroup.

When Matt left for university, I agreed to go out with his best friend. "Going out" soon turned into being a single teenage mum and studying for a criminology exam while nursing my son. That's how I ended up as a young grandma to Becky, who's currently still talking to Matt, even though she must have noticed the direction of his stare.

Time for action. Still no alerts on my phone. I get up and brush an imaginary speck of dust from the sleeve of my work-issue *Ralph Lauren* jacket. When I worked for the Secret

Service, I'd buy my own clothes, and none of them were designer. The private security company looking after the passengers in the Business Lounge makes sure I blend right in.

Nobody could deduce my profession from my attire. Nobody looking at the crinkles around my eyes and lips would ever guess that at the height of my career I prevented seven aeroplane hijacks, four major bombings, and one minor war. Nobody observing me now notices anything except a fellow traveller past her sell-by date.

"Good morning," I say taking the armchair opposite Matt. After almost fifty years, and that's all I have to say to him?

"I wish it was," he replies. His voice is deeper than I remember, full of unfamiliar grooves and cracks. "Delighted to see you, though."

The red rims around his eyes. The clench of the jaw muscles. Becky's business iPad in her lap. I put it all together, turn to my granddaughter. My training takes over. "Salient points?" I ask.

"Thirty-year old male taken hostage on the flight from Johannesburg three hours ago. Travelled with his father." A nod towards Matt. "Went to the bathroom, never came out. The perpetrator is demanding ten million dollars."

The way she said it makes my brain work faster. "Think it's a cover story?"

Matt screws up his face, massages the temples. "I told the negotiator to agree to the demand."

"And?" There'll be time to feel surprise at Matt's multi-millionaire status, but the time is not now.

Becky lifts her eyebrows. "The perp requested a red *Lamborghini* be driven on to the tarmac, the back seat filled with the cash so that he could see it as soon as he disembarked. Deadline," she consults her watch, "forty minutes from now."

A long-forgotten thrill rekindles in my brain, and it has nothing to do with Matt. Well, not exactly, it's his son's life on the line. But I can't afford to engage my emotions. "My experience of luxury cars is somewhat limited, but isn't a *Lamborghini* a two-seater?"

Matt nods, though I can see his heart isn't in the conversation. His knuckles are white. His throat moves as he swallows. "There was a four-seat model back in 2008, and a single-seater five years later."

"One would expect a kidnapper to have thought it through." My mind is racing faster than any *Lamborghini* model. "To have visualised the car and the money. Spotted the logistics problem. Specified a car with a big enough back window, not to mention with a back seat. Or specified the 2008 model if he's set on a *Lamborghini*."

A quick nod from Becky.

"So what does he want?" Matt's voice is soft, lifeless.

Words come to me straight from a superhero movie. "Some men aren't looking for anything logical like money. They can't be bought, bullied, reasoned, or negotiated with. Some men just want to watch the world burn."

"I don't discount your assessment." Matt rubs his temples again. His hair is just as thick as it was at school. "Still, I don't want to take risks. Not a single risk. We'll do it the way the man told us to do it. A red *Lamborghini*. Ten million on the back seat. And absolutely no police involved. Or security. Not even you, Miss," he addresses Becky.

Instantly, I understand three things. One, he loves his son so much, it's clouding his judgement. Two, the reason there's no general alert, is because nobody has dared to go against Matt's wishes. Yet. Three, he doesn't realise what I do for a living.

Becky doesn't need to exchange meaningful glances with me to be on the same page. "I'll organise a clear passage for the car. How are you going to get hold of a *Lamborghini* that's the correct colour, plus all the cash?"

91

I let Matt do the explaining, partly to take his mind off the scenario that's about to play out, and partly to give myself the space to strategize. "Here's what we do," I tell them.

Twenty-five minutes later, we're on the tarmac, next to a red *Lamborghini.* I've borrowed a walking stick and applied grey eyeshadow to my cheeks, achieving a suitably sickly complexion. Matt doesn't need makeup to look shaky and pale. Together, we mount the steps of the aeroplane.

The negotiator's voice sounds in my earpiece. "A passenger has left her pills on the plane," she tells the hostage-taker over their cell phone connection. "She needs them urgently. A matter of life or death. Please come out. The car and cash are waiting for you."

I'm halfway up the steps, with Matt right behind me.

"She's not coming near until I'm out of the airport boundaries," the perp replies.

"Of course not." Calm and reassuring. The negotiator is good at her job. My Becky. I've taught her well.

Matt and I are now all the way up the steps and into the fuselage. We position ourselves outside the First Class toilets.

"We're ready for you," Becky tells the hostage-taker. "The passage is clear."

The door flies open. I glimpse metal against a young man's throat. The perp is surprised to see us, but to him, we're just a couple of old fogeys. His reactions slower than they could have been, I taser him before his sharpened dinner knife makes a mark on Matt's son.

I bend over as much to handcuff the perp as to give father and son a moment for their private reunion.

Becky's waiting outside the plane. One look and Matt's son forgets his recent ordeal.

"You must allow me to buy you dinner," he tells her. "To say thank you for saving my life."

Forget that I was the one using the taser.

Becky takes his arm. "I'm not interested in men," she says kindly. "But please follow me for your medical check-up."

"And you?" Matt asks as they move away.

"Neither am I," I tell him. "Not interested in men, plural. You could twist my arm, though, to generate some curiosity about one particular man."

"Twist your arm? You mean, like this?"

Oh. He really does twist my arm behind my back. It's not painful at all, but even with all my training, I can't break loose. Not that I care to, because the familiar angles of his body are pressing into my curves, and I can smell the lemony pine of his childhood shampoo. Memories burst through the dams I built over the years. Matt teaching me the map of the stars. Matt learning the steps of the waltz. Matt keeping me warm that time we got lost on the summer school camp.

"You're not the only one with a secret past," he teases.

"What did you used to be before you got super rich? *Batman*?"

"*Batman is* super rich. Doesn't stop him being *Batman*. No, I was a firefighter."

"A trouble shooter? Like, in the business world?"

"No. Like a fireman. In a burning house."

Do not think about calendar photos of men in red trucks with no shirts on. Do not think... No good. I'm thinking about Matt without his shirt on. Next to a red fire truck. Leaning on a red *Lamborghini*. Carrying a pretty redhead out of a flaming inferno.

How did I ever fool myself into believing I didn't like Matt "in that way"?

"A real hero, then," I manage to articulate with my mouth that's suddenly dry. "Beats a superhero any day."

He still hasn't let go of me. "You weren't too bad yourself." His lips are right by my ear. "Your daughter told me a few details that would make *Super Girl* turn the colour of *The Hulk* with envy."

"Granddaughter," I correct automatically.

Now he does release his grip, spins me around. "You really didn't wait around when I left."

My cheeks must resemble *The Flash's* costume. "More the fool, me."

"No." Matt lifts my chin with his thumb. "More the fool, me."

My mouth is a finger's width away from his. The world is standing still. I wonder what superheroes do when they retire. And I have no doubt I'm about to find out.

Never Have I Ever

Never have I ever expected a message from him. Eight years after school graduation. I mean, it's not like we've ever been an item. Not even good friends.

"Leonie, hi, hope u remember me," he says in his text. "I'm in town. U free 2 meet 2nite?"

As it happens, I'm not. My nights are bursting with Pilates, book club, chick flick, volunteering at the old age home. Married colleagues tell me these are all meaningless activities we singles use to pretend we have a life. They don't understand it's a choice: a tidy apartment with my things arranged the way I want them. My schedule. My holiday plans. My way.

Plus, I totally hate the way he texted – with numbers and simplified spelling. That's H-A-T-E, not H-8.

So I hesitate. I um and ah over the reply during a pointless marketing meeting. Theo. He's nearly a year younger than me. At school, when we were seventeen, the age gap was a chasm.

I wonder whether it matters now we're eight years older. I'm curious why he remembers me and how he got my number. (My Mum? Dad?) Plus, I'm dying to know what he looks like. Back then, he was still playing catch-up. No pimples, no facial hair, no Adam's apple. No bad language, no sleazy comments, no leers…

"Okay," I type back. "I'll cancel my flying lesson."

He thinks it's a joke.

"Ten more hours in the air and I'll have my private pilot licence." No idea why I tell him. It's not like I'm trying to impress him, even though his *Facebook* profile (no photo) says he's a film producer in Los Angeles. Another text vibrates my phone. "What else don't I know about you?"

At least no abbreviations this time.

Where to begin? Since leaving school I've obtained a degree and changed careers. I've seen friends get married, get heartbroken, get divorced. They didn't have my parents as examples of what not to do. Rule number one: don't fall in love. Rule number two: ever.

"Not sure what to tell you. Eight years is a long time."

"Enough to write 275 Beatles songs," he replies. "And no, I'm not a *Trivial Pursuit* geek. I've googled it."

This makes me smile, and suddenly I can't wait for five pm. My face upturned towards the graph of our customers' demographics, I frown slightly as though taking in the percentages, while typing into my phone under the table. "Let's play 'never have I ever'. We can do the penalty drinks when we meet."

While I wait for Theo's reply, I assess my surroundings. I see my boss nod with approval when the new slide appears, so I nod, too.

"Questions?" asks the presenter.

I'm good with numbers, so I risk it. "Aren't the teenage market sales up significantly this quarter?"

The boss beams at me. Others race to outshine me by suggesting reasons for the increase, so I look at my phone.

"Never have I ever played this game," Theo says. "Only seen it on TV. *The Big Bang Theory. Lost.*"

I love both shows. "You win this round," I tell him. "Never have I ever regretted being single."

"Tricky. I like relationships. But I don't think I've ever regretted my patches of un-attachment. Better to be alone than settle for second-best, right?" Good old romantic Theo. "My turn. Never have I ever had a one-night stand."

Well, if he still looks like Bambi, all innocent and adolescent, perhaps girls are too scared to hurt his feelings with a one-off? "I've only ever had one-night stands." I reply. "Never have I ever had a second date."

96

"Really?"

Really. I don't do second dates. Mostly, my first dates are either spectacular disasters or disastrously boring. The few that go all right scare me right off, although some end with a one-night stand. Okay, two so far.

I'm not proud of that, it's just the way it worked out. In those good-date moments, I think a relationship might be on the cards. Not marriage, of course. Not earth-shattering love. Just potential. A possibility of companionship, shared memories. Something.

And then, in the cold light of a new day, I feel a wall of ice growing around my heart. The internet tells me my commitment phobia can be traced back to my insecure childhood in an unstable home. I tell myself it's because I'm happy to be single, and that I don't need a man to make me complete.

Theo's contribution buzzes in. "Never have I ever sexted anyone I wasn't attracted to."

Wait. Is he trying to say he finds me attractive? Is he flirting with me?

A sudden memory lodges itself like a splinter in my conscience. A school sports event. Me – trying to get another boy's attention. Theo – sitting behind me in the grandstand. I nudged him. "Uncomfortable," I told him. "I'm going to lean against your knees." Then, after a while, "Your knees are uncomfortable, too. Open them." Yeah, that's how innocent I was back then. I ended up resting my head on Theo's stomach, my shoulders between his thighs.

A wave of heat threatens to colour my face. In my defence, he wasn't boyfriend material. More like a younger brother. I stifle the – now erotic – image and join the marketing discussion with another data-related comment.

Time to dial the conversation down to less personal. "Never have I ever made a movie."

"Cheat! But I'll let you have it. Never have I ever published any statistical analysis of anything."

Right, so he has googled me, too.

"Send me your photo," I type. "In case I don't recognise you when we meet."

Glad I've asked. The picture that fills the phone's screen bears only the slightest resemblance to the Theo I remember.

Gone are the glasses. The baby-bottom skin is weathered by the outdoors, the forehead is etched by life's trials. The smile is still the same, now framed with a dark smudge of stubble. And yup, the line of his throat is broken by a masculine Adam's apple.

Wow. Today's Theo looks... looks... just wow.

Perhaps I shouldn't be meeting him, after all.

I'm happy being single, I'm happy being single, I repeat the mantra.

Finally, the sales presentation is over, bang on five pm, and I purposefully don't brush my hair or re-powder my nose. My place of work frowns on makeup, so I'm going to meet Theo looking as natural as sunlight on the bay. No lipstick. No mascara. No pretence. And no chance of a second date. That's the way I want to play it.

"You haven't changed," I hear behind me. Behind me... and way, way above.

I turn, glance up. Theo is... he's... tall. No, *tall* is an understatement. Back at school, we were the same height. Now my nose reaches the lower edge of his breastbone. His chest and shoulders are twice as broad as I remember.

This is the guy I used to lean in against while watching school athletics? Be still my hormones.

"You haven't changed a bit either," I quip. "So, what's the score in our 'never have I ever' game?"

"Enough to get us both drunk. Feel like getting drunk?"

"Not especially." Never have I ever been drunk, a glass of wine usually lasts me a whole evening, but I don't tell him that.

We agree that the bar is too noisy and crowded, and the movies are not the best setting for a conversation to span eight years. Before he mentions dinner – way, way too much commitment so early in the evening – I suggest tenpin bowling.

The good thing about bowling alleys is that they're brightly lit, gaudy, and not at all romantic. At six o'clock, they're also pretty deserted.

Theo tells me about his filming projects. It's reality TV. At first, I'm disappointed it's not blockbuster movies, but the passionate way he talks about each series makes me realise his programmes might be kind of cool. Travel. Investigating conspiracy theories. There is this one show, think *Dr Phil* meets *Lost*, in which a couple on the brink of divorce is thrown into an extreme survival situation on a tropical island. I almost wish this programme had been around twenty years ago, and that my parents were on it. When a marriage is in dire straits, reality TV hardly seems like an answer, and yet having to forage for food could have done more for Mum and Dad than the communications course their therapist insisted on.

We bowl and chat, chat and bowl. I change the ball's weight four times. I experiment with hard straight throws and soft zig-zaggy ones.

"You know what I admire about you?" Theo asks when I get a strike.

"Everything?"

"True. Right now, though, I admire that you always know what you want and you go after it. Be it a strike or emotional independence. Or that guy at school, what was his name? Perry? Percy?"

"Pierce." Does Theo remember that day in the grandstand? Heat floods my cheeks. "Your turn to bowl."

Theo kills eight pegs. "You went out with him in the end, didn't you?"

"Once. I don't do second dates, remember?"

"Then we've hit a conundrum."

"A conundrum," I repeat.

Theo lifts his hand in a "wait" gesture, pulls out his phone and types. I like it that he's using a sliding keyboard: his moves are elegant and minimalistic. A text buzzes in my handbag. I retrieve it.

"Never have I ever had a first date that didn't result in a second."

I consider texting back, but I'm in too much of a hurry. "What if this isn't a date?"

Theo arches his eyebrows. He has good eyebrows: dark and thick and broad. "What is it then?"

"Two old school mates meeting up."

He considers it. "Can the two old school mates meet up again next week? I have to fly back to put my project to bed, but I can be back by Friday."

"That'll work for me," I say, and the swiftness of my reply scares me. "I'll cancel my pole-dancing class."

His expression makes me long for next Friday.

"Not a joke," I assure him. "It's good exercise."

Theo assumes a mock-preachy pose. "Please don't skip your exercise routine on my account. Your health is too important to toy with. I'll come watch your class."

He will? My mind flits from Big-Boobs-Bianca to Long-Legged Letitia.

No. Frigging. Way. Theo's mine. Can't believe it's taken me eight years to see it.

"Tell you what," I say. "When the two old school mates meet for the tenth time, I'll give you a private pole-dancing demonstration."

The gleam in Theo's eyes tells me he'll be counting.

Friend Now Greeting Foe

<<< Dust. Heat. The smell of diesel and sweat. The Humvee stops. Through the fissure in the rocks, I glimpse a female face. Toffee-skinned like all the Afghani, yet eyes unlike any I've ever seen. Feral, wolf-like, green-gold. Mesmerising. I can't move. I can't look away. >>>

The 3D monitor flickered. *Blink. Blink. Blink.*

"See that?" The radiologist pointed. "Your baby's heartbeat."

My wife's fingers interlaced with mine. Not the most comfortable position for my wrist, but I would get used to it. I had to get used to a lot now that I was a civilian again. A civilian. A married man. A father-to-be.

Her voice brimmed over with tenderness. "Oh, my. Wow."

I merely nodded. Didn't have the words. My baby's heart pulsated on the screen, every thud a tiny explosion. As an ex-soldier, I knew about explosions.

Blink, blink, blink, went the screen. I blinked back. Men don't cry. Not war heroes, at any rate.

I had returned home a month after NATO carved out the peace settlement with the Taliban. Like the politicians, I did not return from Afghanistan empty-handed. The politicians brought back the soldiers and enough borrowed money to pull the world out of the recession. I brought back my bride.

Fareiba's name means "very pretty", and that's an understatement. With her eyes green and full of fire, her beauty has a wild-animal quality. I was smitten the moment I met her. Me, an English soldier falling for an Afghani girl. Just like that Roger Whittaker song, you know the one that talks about friend now greeting foe, that's how it was with us. Yesterday's enemies, today's newlyweds. Irony, right?

My folks were none too happy at first. Nor at second. Nor ever, to be honest. A foreign daughter-in-law meant foreign customs, a foreign language, a foreign God. Their son, the war hero, should have done better.

The hero thing was exaggerated, a matter of being in the right place at the right time. Fareiba spotted me in the *Humvee* heading for a trap and hesitated a moment too long before detonating the explosives. Love at first sight, everybody said later. However it came about, though, the important bit was she was going to kill me, and she didn't. Instead, she started working with us. Told us the where and the when of the future attacks. Told us the weak spots. Told us how to get them where it hurt. At the time we had no idea who she was nor how valuable the information was. Bit by bit, though, we more or less forced the Taliban to the negotiation table.

Fareiba said she'd done it because she was sick of the war. War happens because one high-on-power individual designates the enemy and decides they have to be vanquished. No matter how just the cause though, she'd said, nothing can justify one stranger killing another for the sin of being born into another nation.

She'd said all that, and her hot green eyes never left my face. A week later, we were married. And yet, even when our love story became the symbol of peace in every media outlet, my folks still disapproved.

Perhaps the baby would change their minds.

"We'll just run the usual tests," the radiologist said.

I wasn't concerned. Our baby was conceived by young and genetically diverse parents. What could possibly go wrong?

<<< Dust. Heat. The smell of diesel and sweat and fear. "The Ish Pesta road is blocked," the driver calls. "We have to make a detour."

I still can't take my eyes off the woman. She's young, younger than me, yet I would never call her a girl. Her green eyes have witnessed too much, lost their innocence to the ravages of war.

Something happens inside my chest. At first I think a bullet or a piece of shrapnel. Pain. Feels a bit like injury and a bit like a mutation. I'm not the same person I was a second before I'd seen those green-gold eyes. My head feels weightless. My heart is pounding. Is that what love at first sight feels like?

I want to get to know her. Smell her hair, taste her mouth, feel her hips against mine. Love, lust, what's the difference, really? You can dress up the yearning any way you like, it all comes down to biology and procreation.

The woman lifts her arm. That's when I know. A trap. An IED. An improvised explosive device. A roadside bomb.

When you're in the war zone, reality is enhanced. Colours are more colourful, the heat is hotter, a broken heart more agonizing. In the war zone, only this existence is real.

What's back home is an illusion. Back home is irrelevant, for how can it compare with the life-death actuality of war? >>>

When I got back home from the war, reality felt more authentic. Colours were less vivid yet more life-like, the temperature more temperate, decisions easier to make: flat white or cappuccino, blue t-shirt or black, to have or not to have the 12-weeks Downs Syndrome scan.

The radiologist's face resembled that of a poker player. I had played enough back at the base to recognise that total deliberate blanking of the eyes and forced relaxing of the jaw. "Let's just do one more measurement," he said, positioning the sensor over Fareiba's abdomen.

"Problem?" If there was one, I wanted to know straight away. That's army training for you. Emotions could kill you. You learnt to deal with facts and solutions.

The radiologist cut his gaze from me to Fareiba, then to me again. "Not to worry."

The lie slithered out of his mouth, white and big as an elephant. Fareiba didn't notice, she just closed her eyes and exhaled with relief you could lay a hand on. I couldn't believe it that Fareiba, my Fareiba, the woman trained in undercover and counter-intelligence work, Taliban's top female agent, could fall for the fib so easily. Guess we all believe what we want to believe, what we *need* to believe in a life-death situation.

<<< Dust. Heat. The smell of diesel and sweat and fear and explosives. I don't hear the bang. All I know is, I'm flying through the air. An angel. A dove of peace. Icarus.

My spine hits the ground. A fallen angel. A dead peace offering. A boy who tried too hard to please.

My great-grandfather gave five years of his life and both legs to his country during the Second World War. Our family never forgot. And so I joined the army to pay the debt, to do my share, and, if truth be told, to earn some of that luminous patina of heroism. How was I to know there was nothing heroic about shooting at fellow humans and getting blown up?

The woman is still there, in the rock fissure now splattered with blood. Does she – even now – hold on to her illusions of being a hero and saving her country?

She's watching me. Green – such an unusual colour for eyes, particularly in Afghanistan. Is there sadness in them? Regret? I can't see it. I can't see anything. >>>

"The nuchal folds are measuring within the norm," the radiologist said.

I wasn't buying it. Life's never this easy. "You sure?"

"Upper limit, but within the norm. Given the young age of the mother, I wouldn't worry."

I did worry. Couldn't help it. Silence filled the room, deafening in its absence of sound. My baby, a pulse on the computer screen, an imperceptible knoll on Fareiba's belly.

"Do the blood test." My wife's soft, stable voice echoed like a detonation. A true soldier, this one.

"Gather information, formulate a tactical plan, act it out?" I joked, though laughter was the last thing my constricted lungs could manage.

"That's the idea." She didn't smile, either. Her green eyes were closed, her lips moving as if in prayer.

What would our tactical plan involve if the baby didn't have the correct number of chromosomes? Raise a handicapped child whose life expectancy meant we would probably outlive it? Or kill it now, before we got to know it and love it?

I'd killed before, so I knew this much: killing was killing, regardless of whether you killed an insurgent or a foetus. Foetus. Insurgent. It was just a word play, a deft way of dehumanising the victim. Back in the army though, you just followed orders. Back in the army, the blood of the dead wasn't on your hands. Here, it would be our decision. Our hands. Our baby's blood.

Panic, unlike any I'd ever known, not even by that rock face on the way to Ish Pesta, gripped my throat.

"Earth to Ralph?"

"I'm here, honey." A fib. My mind was back in the war zone, my nostrils almost filled with Afghanistan's dry dusty heat.

A nurse entered the room. "It's a privilege to meet you both," she said. Her cheekbones went pink, then crimson.

Huh? I didn't get it at first. Her star-struck hero-worship expression enlightened me. "Oh." I shrugged. "Don't believe everything you read in the newspapers. War is evil."

"War is a necessary evil." The nurse inserted the needle into my wife's arm. "Without the navy, we would never have discovered the uses of ultrasound, and we wouldn't be able to do your prenatal screening today."

Was prenatal screening a blessing or a burden? I held Fareiba's cool hand in my sweaty one while the blood poured out of her vein into the glass tube. In that instant, I knew I would gladly give my own blood, all of it, in exchange for our baby's life.

Nothing heroic in that. Sheer animal instinct. Evolution at its purest.

There Must Be an App for That!

90 Days to Go

Extra, extra, read all about it! Guess it's not news to you, as this blog is titled *Mother-Of-The-Bride*, but I confess my eyes were damp and my throat tight when Megan showed me the ring. Magnificent.

Not that the size of the diamond matters. What counts is that Megan and Tom are crazy about each other, that Tom has his own start-up business and no body piercings. And his mum is lovely, too. Megan won't have any mother-in-law dramas.

My baby's getting married. The date's only three months away! How is a single parent supposed to organise a formal white wedding all by herself? There must be an app for that!

89 Days to Go

Not formal white. Megan wants to do this sustainable-earth stuff. I called Tom's mum, and at the end of the hour-long chat I have two phone-screen scrolls' worth of ideas: cotton-fibre wedding invitations, organic buffet, edible confetti, a barn setting.

Of all the wedding planning apps available, I'm using three of them. I want to make sure I cannot forget a thing. This way, I can share the plans with Tom's mum. I should stop calling her that, shouldn't I? Libby. Her name's Libby.

88 Days to Go

Apparently no more sustainable-earth stuff. Goth is the latest flavour. That means Megan's planning to wear black. *Black*! What is she thinking? What kind of a message will a bride in mourning send to the guests and groom?

87 Days to Go

Megan's reminded me that I wore virginal white and look how my marriage's turned out. Meeow! Surely there must be an app available that comes up with clever rejoinders. Or at least an app that manages grown-up daughters who still sound like teenagers.

I know, I know. My fault that Megan and I never got around to ironing out the little (and not so little) crinkles our relationship sustained in the warzone of Megan's coming of age. Result? A twenty-five-year old woman going on fifteen whenever her mum's around.

If only she could feel how much I love her. If only she knew how desolate the distance between us makes me. If only there was something I could do.

That's why I'm sending out eighteen wedding invitations written with white ink on black. We shared the list and Libby is doing twenty-two for her side of the family.

86 Days to Go

Question: what's the etiquette around inviting your ex to your child's wedding? Really? That he left us five years ago and didn't send as much as a text is irrelevant? Drat.

Dimitri and I had both just turned twenty-one when we tied the knot. Megan was a flower-girl at our wedding, looking exquisite in her white pouffy dress, her three-year-old mouth round with concentration. No wonder she doesn't want a pouffy white dress now. The way my marriage went, thank goodness she wants a husband.

Those first years after Megan's birth were tough. A screaming baby is a danger to any relationship, but particularly to a teenage one. Yet we survived the marital quarrels, the nappies, the terrible-twos and the worse-thirteens.

Dimitri left us when the going finally got good: with the mortgage paid off and Megan at university. I suggested we do a bit of travelling, Paris maybe, to renew our vows. That's when he told me he was leaving, because I was too "egotistic and self-absorbed". Only, the red-headed woman who drove him and his five suitcases away from our family home couldn't have been much older than our daughter. Afterwards, I found out the redhead had been one of many.

Thus, egotistically and self-absorbedly, I don't want to see Dimitri ever again. Not even at Megan's wedding.

Libby has it easy. Her ex is dead... I didn't mean that. It was traumatic for her, and worse for Tom. Sometimes, though, it's easier to mourn a good man than to forgive a bad one.

Still, he's Megan's dad. Megan, a tiny bump in my teenage tummy and a huge bump in my life's journey. Megan, three-point-five kilograms of pinkness that smelled of sweet almonds and bawled like a banshee. Megan, the ungainly teen, the elegant young woman. I'd walk through fire for her, give up my life to save hers, buy her a happily-ever-after app even if it cost my own comfort.

Dimitri never left me his new address, but Mr Google knows everything. With fingers that don't cooperate, I write out the nineteenth invitation.

Megan will have Daddy walk her down the aisle.

84 Days to Go

Disaster! My sister has just split up with her husband. I know about the fragility of marriage vows first-hand, but seriously? Seriously?

"You can't do this to me," I wail when she phones.

"I've already mailed your wedding invitation. Addressed to both of you."

Right, so perhaps I can be a bit "egotistic and self-absorbed" at times.

My sister offers no apology. "I'll white-out his name and write *plus-one* if it makes you feel better."

White-out won't work, I want to tell her. Better use tar. Or black nail polish. Megan and I bought four bottles yesterday.

"Do you have a *plus-one*?" The question slips out before I can swallow it.

"Darling, I have a *plus-five. Plus-ten.* You wouldn't believe the selection out here if you…"

I say goodbye before she has a chance to broach the taboo topic. After Dimitri, the idea of trusting another man with my brittle self-confidence is about as appealing as having open-heart surgery without an anaesthetic.

70 Days to Go

Today I purchased a mother-of-the-bride outfit. That's the third one now. So, decision time. The silk black one, dressed up with jewellery? Methinks I'd need a lot of jewellery to stand out in the crowd of black: black bride, black groom, black bridesmaids.

The two-piece sea-blue suit then? Hmmm. It makes me look like the Queen -and not *a queen* if you see the difference.

Or this latest purchase, the liquid gold draping my waist and falling just so around the hips?

"The gold," Libby says. "It highlights your colouring. Plus, by the time you're done making all the silk flowers, you'll never want to look at silk again."

She has a point. The table centrepieces are ready, but Megan's bouquet and the arrangements for the aisle are still on the to-do list, in three list apps, no less, while I'm choosing between them.

Must remember to book the band.

69 Days to Go

No venue yet. So far, Megan's vetoed my every suggestion: a vineyard, a church, our garden, the beach. It so reminds me of planning her tenth birthday party, I actually mention a steam train and a trampoline hall.

Idea: move the whole wedding to a faraway exotic location, like Singapore's *Raffles* hotel. Megan in a long white dress would descend the sweeping staircase into the marble lobby… Oh, wait. Not white. Black.

Black, with one thousand fake black pearls that I'm to sew onto it. I doubt there's an app for that.

67 Days to Go

Dimitri emailed to accept the wedding invitation. Said he wouldn't be bringing a plus-one.

You know, I kind of feel sorry for the redhead.

63 Days to Go

Megan's approved a traditional fruitcake, as long as it's iced black, with red roses on top. Having perused images of Goth weddings on the net, I'm thankful she doesn't want a crow, caskets, or garlands of dripping blood.

The wedding décor is to run all crisp black, vivid reds, and glittering crystal. The reception hall, however, will be covered in cobwebs and artificial fog. Clearly, not enough Halloween parties in Megan's childhood. There must be an app for making spooky ornaments.

Libby says Tom's happy with whatever wedding theme Megan picks. He's taking care of the honeymoon. The arrangements are so top secret that even Libby has no idea. The brochures he leaves around cover everything from Fiji to Alaska.

My little girl. On a honeymoon.

Seems like only a few years ago she was playing weddings with *Barbie* and *Ken*. The dolls would speed away in a pink car towards their bright future under the dining room chair.

That reminds me. I was fully prepared to oppose hiring a hearse, but – thank heavens – Megan's going with white stretch limos. All booked and paid for in advance, before she changes her mind.

30 Days to Go

Love is… sewing on 816 black pearls onto a black wedding dress.

Libby does the other 184. Says it would be a waste if the mother of the bride went blind from all the needlework and didn't get to see the wedding.

21 Days to Go

Dimitri phones to ask what gift to bring. I say Megan only needs him. His voice, once so much part of my life, confuses the past and the present. I can't decipher the emotions clutching at my throat.

10 Days to Go

What am I forgetting?

Hairdresser, check. Photographer, check. Caterer, check. Newspaper announcement?

Libby is a rock. She's keeping me sane.

Blast Off!

And here we are, in a disused Victorian theatre, under a crystal chandelier, among the black-and-red silk flowers I had to re-attach with a glue gun at the last minute because they threatened to fall apart in the heat.

Megan is looking stunning. Black suits her. Being the centre of attention suits her. Love suits her best of all. My love, and Dimitri's, but above all Tom's.

"I will never betray you, for you are my heart, my soul and my life."

I cry.

1 Day After

It's over. The newlyweds arrived safely in Singapore's *Raffles* and are basking in opulence. Tom says I gave him the idea.

Libby and I are enjoying coffee in my garden, when... I can't believe it... Dimitri walks through the gate, dimples in his cheeks, and falls to his knees.

"Let's start again. Renew our vows in Paris. Exactly like you wanted."

Like I wanted five long years ago. I'm tempted to ask whatever happened to *egotistic* and *self-absorbed*, but, honestly, what's the point? There must be an app for forgiveness. It's just that I don't have it installed.

"We will never have Paris," I tell him, a little sorry. For him, for the *us* we once were, for the future we won't have. But mostly, because I do want to see Paris. Just not with Dimitri.

With Libby.

The realisation jolts me. Libby?

In a kaleidoscope of memory fragments, I relive the last

three months. Sampling seven wedding cakes together, laughing in the shoe shops, having our nails done. Talking, and finishing each other's thoughts.

My eyes find hers. Predictably – she already knows.

I've always considered myself straight, yet I feel no need to re-label. Not gay, not straight. Just two women in love going to Paris.

So simple I don't need an app for it.

The Day the Internet Died, Maybe

When it comes to computer games, you think you've seen it all. Dragons, droids, wizards, warriors. Even the legendary landscape of planet Pandora.

Yet you've seen nothing until you've been to Like Life.

Matt Fisher was not a loser. He had a job he didn't hate. He had a house that didn't leak. He'd never done anything likely to get him arrested. An image consultant would call him single, with a steady job, and a starter home ready for a family. But then an image consultant would also spike his hair and throw away his baggy trousers.

Matt Fisher could have spent a lot of money on image.

Instead, he spent it on a game of the newly released *Like Life*.

Imagine you are who you want to be, exactly who you've always wanted to be. You are Matt Fisher the prince, Matt Fisher the poet, Matt Fisher a scholar and a sportsman and a superhero.

You live in a mansion on your own private island, or a penthouse apartment in New York. You can invite Miss Universe to join you for a drink, or have a few mates over for a night of cigars and poker, or both.

In Like Life not even the sky is the limit. Because Like Life is not like your life at all. It's like nothing you've ever experienced in your wildest fantasies. It's your whole life now. And it's about to crash.

Matt Fisher could have invited Miss Universe to join him for a drink, but he didn't think of it. He could have had a few mates for a boys' night in, but he didn't think of it, either. Matt Fisher enjoyed his own company.

The shock, when it came, was not because the internet crashed, taking *Like Life* down with it – it was because Matt found himself face to face with a woman. She had pink-rimmed glasses, pink hair, and pink chewing gum.

"Are you still connected?" The girl's voice wasn't exactly pink, but it could've been. The chewing gum popped out in a pink bubble, grew larger and thinner, contorting the girl's features like a funfair mirror. "Is your internet up?"

Matt shrugged. They were in an internet café, his regular lunchtime spot ever since his office's network blocked *Like Life*. Easy enough to see that every computer was off-line. Let the pink girl put two and two together herself.

He became aware of other voices around them.

"Does *Gmail* auto-save draft messages?"

"Damn, I was three-quarters of the way through my grocery shopping."

"The auction closes in seven minutes! Should have auto-bid…"

"Anybody got today's weather report? I crashed before I got there."

"The weather report? Just look out the window, mate."

"Hey, you!" The pink girl jabbed her pink fingernail at Matt's chest. "Are you listening to me?"

"No." Automatic, defensive.

She smiled. "Gotcha."

The café owner shouted over the din. "Not just the café's connection. It's everybody."

A small voice splintered the sudden silence. "You mean the whole city?"

"Could be bigger. I haven't…"

Matt tuned out. Pulled out his phone to call the office – they, too, were cut off. The phone's browser confirmed his growing fear there was no connection.

"Hey." The pink girl again. "I've just called Europe and America. Their internet's vanished, just like ours."

Matt stared at her.

The pink girl blew another pink bubble at him. "Say something."

Why didn't she just go away? Honestly, how was he supposed to react? Eventually, he settled for "Okay."

"Okay? Okay? Is that all you have?"

"Yes." He gave her flat eyes, hoping she'd get the hint.

She didn't. Her pink glasses twinkled in the fluorescent light of the café. "Come on then. Let's go fix it."

Fix it? Was she nuts?

Aloud he said, "I'm sure they have people working on it."

Whoever *they* were. As much as Matt loved the internet, he never bothered to find out how it all ran. It ran was the main thing, the only thing. Only now, it ran... not.

The pink eyebrows shot up. "They do indeed. I'm the *people* they have working on it. Name's Jane, by the way. Jane Lockwood."

Jane? How could anything so pink and sparkly be called plain Jane?

"What's yours?"

"Matt. Fisher."

She extended her hand. Matt had no choice but to shake it. It was like shaking a piece of fillet steak. Human contact. Who needed it, right? In future, he'd stick to *Facebook*, online chats and – yeah – *Like Life*.

Jane, meanwhile, kept talking. He caught the last bit.

"We have a good chance," she punctuated every phrase with an exclamation mark. "I'm in general troubleshooting now, but I used to work for the company who maintains the cables."

"What cables?"

117

"The underwater ones that connect the continents."

"There are cables?" Somehow Matt had imagined a wireless connection across the oceans.

"Yeah. There's a snag, though." More bubble gum balloons. "The undersea cables come from all over. Now, for the whole of the internet to crash like this, most of the cables would have to be cut."

Matt didn't care. He just wanted back into the virtual reality. If he could afford it, he'd never come out of *Like Life*. Not go to work. Not shower. He'd pay somebody to feed him, or he'd connect himself to intravenous tubing.

Now, for the first time, he imagined what his life would be like without the game. The grey routine of it, the pointlessness of life without *Like Life* punched a hole in his chest, made his lungs work overtime.

"I need to get back in." The words grated his throat on the way out.

She just stood there, looking pink.

"Okay," he said. "So there are too many cables to cut. What else could have caused the crash?"

"A solar flare. A hack-attack. A political directive."

Hopeless. It was all hopeless. How can you fight a solar flare? "What can we do?"

"Let's go fix it," she said. She pointed to the café customers, who now yelled obscenities and hit the top of their terminal screens. "Before civilisation as we know it comes to an end."

If it weren't for Jane, Matt knew, he would have been pounding the dead computer along with the rest of them. He followed the pink ponytail out onto the street, his brain pounding. How on earth was she going to counteract a solar flare?

The pink ponytail swerved. "I don't know what's wrong but I do know how to fix it. In England, at least, not sure about the rest of the world."

Matt didn't give a ferret's whisker about the rest of the world.

"Are you with me, Matt?"

Anything to get back to his paradise island. "Yeah."

"Good. What we need to do, is connect up the backup and reboot the internet. Some data will be lost, of course…"

"How much data?"

"Everything since three in the morning. That's when we back up the system."

Matt chewed on this. Everything from his morning session of *Like Life*, plus what he achieved this lunchtime. Annoying, but not shattering.

He could feel the tension seep out of his shoulders. "What are you going to do?"

"Me?" Her laughter was pink and bubbly, like the rest of her. "It's your job, super hero."

No. No way. He was so not a hero. "Tell me what to do."

The rest felt like a dream. Not in an *it's-so-wonderful* sense, more like *this-is-so-not-real*. The drive to Jane's house. The frantic powering up of what looked like very large hard disks. The part where it needed two people to turn keys and type in codes, the one that looked like a bad Stop-World-War-Three movie.

"That was fun," Jane high-fived him. Her touch should have been abhorrent. It wasn't. "How did you like it, Matt Fisher? Doing stuff in the real world?"

Fun? Matt shrugged. "I guess."

"How about a *Coke* to celebrate?" Jane's glasses glimmered more of their pink magic. "We can sit down and…"

Too much too fast. "Nah. Let's go back to the café and wait for the net to wake up."

"Like *Sleeping Beauty*? Perhaps it's waiting for a kiss from a handsome prince?"

Honestly! Was she for real? He backed out of her house. "The café," he said.

They drove back in silence, entered the café without looking at each other. The chirp of Jane's phone was like the sound of a win on an electronic slot machine. She listened, looked up, all pink and smiley. "The internet is up, folks. Sorry for the inconvenience."

All around them, people looked up, nodded, then... Matt couldn't believe his eyes... they all returned to drinking coffee and talking. Auctions lay forgotten, emails downgraded in urgency. Everyone was just... in the moment.

"Hey. Earth to Matt Fisher."

He glanced up into eyes framed by pink lashes. Jane pressed something rectangular into his hand.

"My card. Call me some time," she said. "Otherwise we will have fixed the internet for nothing."

Had they really fixed the internet, though? Or was the whole mini-quest just Jane's impromptu scheme to get to know him better? Perhaps she'd seen him here before. Perhaps she thought an internet café was as good a place as a dating site. What was real, really? Matt didn't know.

"Matt?"

Matt looked at Jane. He looked at the computer. They'd been through so much, his computer and Matt. He wasn't going to waste it on pink girls.

Lunchtime was almost over, but he could squeeze in another five minutes. Heck, he could take the rest of the afternoon off.

He logged into *Like Life*.

The pink girl was waiting for him on his island. Except here she wasn't pink, she was a blonde, which made her much more realistic. The sun-drenched deck chair creaked as she leaned forward.

"Fancy a game of *Halo*?" she asked.

Matt nodded approval. She hadn't offered him a *Coke* – she'd suggested a game. In *Like Life*, Jane really knew him.

You think you've seen it all. Dragons, droids, wizards, warriors. Even the legendary landscape of planet Pandora.

You've seen nothing until you've been to Like Life.

The Volcano Blast Party

The car radio's fifteen speakers blasted out something that tried hard *not* to be a warning.

"*...The latest series of tremors in the Auckland region,*" said the reporter, "*is not, I repeat, is not indicative of a new volcano forming in the Hauraki Gulf. The scientists...*"

Josh wasn't buying it for a moment, though he knew his father would gather up the family and run somewhere safe. Escape was his father's solution to everything. Run away and wait it out.

The trouble was that, at seventeen, Josh was sick of safe.

This was one of the reasons he was doing 150km/h in an 80km/h zone.

"*...Greater Auckland is not sufficiently equipped to deal with the hypothetical emergency of a volcanic eruption. The traffic congestion resulting from any evacuation, forced or voluntary...*"

His phone rang with the beat of tribal drums. One glance at the caller ID was enough to make his heartbeat race. "Yo, Zoë," he said, keeping his emotions in check. Then, before he could bite off his tongue, "Long time."

A fraction of silence, as tense as the rubber in a condom put on to your face for a laugh after you've had far too many.

Then Zoë's matter-of-fact tone, "We're having a Volcano Blast Emergency party tonight. Interested?"

"Yeah." An understatement of the millennium.

"The thing is..." Zoë paused.

"Yeah?" That's good. If he kept to monosyllables, perhaps he wouldn't make a fool of himself.

"The thing is location."

His chest tightened. She only phoned because she needed a place for the party.

Stop it. She phoned.

"No prob. You... we can have it at mine," he said.

"Wicked! See you around eight then?"

"You bet."

Suddenly it felt so very good to be alive.

"...How would your family deal with food shortages, drain blockage, contamination of drinking water, disruption to electricity and phone..."

His family knew exactly how to deal with all of that. When he got home, a packed suitcase awaited him.

"We're leaving for Sydney after lunch," his mother said. "Your father wants to take the jet. It gives us more options."

Josh shrugged. "The boat is bigger and more comfortable."

"The boat might not outrun the tsuna..."

She broke off and pressed her lips together for a brief moment, then stretched them out in a big cheerful smile.

The plane, the boat – it didn't matter to Josh either way. Let his father throw money at the problem, all his easily earned millions.

Josh had other plans.

Nianzu watched as the rich white man locked the gate and set the perimeter beams that would comb the garden for intruders in the family's absence.

"Hurry up, Dad!"

The son and daughter of the rich white man sat side by side at the back of the BMW. They just sat there, with no earphones on their ears, or palmtops in their palms. Their inactivity was unusual. Most Western teenagers nowadays didn't know how to keep their mouths quiet and their bodies calm without an electronic gadget.

"Honey, did you remember to cancel the newspaper?"

The wife was at the wheel, her face – still pretty – now distorted by the way she kept pressing her lips into one another. Her unease was also out of the ordinary.

Today, they did not look the way they had the last three – or was it four – times that Nianzu had broken into their mansion. Today, they did not look like a family going on holiday at all, even though the autumn cold had already turned the trees to brown and it was time for this particular family to fly away to warmer climates.

It was also time for his family to find a home for the winter. The minute the BMW disappeared around the corner, Nianzu inserted a thin metal file into the gate. Next he disabled the perimeter beams and the motion sensors (compliments of sweat-shopping for an alarm manufacturer back in his homeland).

"Greetings to you, oh Spirits of this House," chanted Mei as she followed him into the hallway. "We come in peace."

"We come in need," echoed Nianzu. "Be kind to us."

They burned incense and tied a red ribbon on the front door for good luck. The evil was now purged from the house.

The same could not be said about the evil in their memories.

"It's all because of our daughter-in-law," sighed Mei as soon as the cleansing ritual was over. "She doesn't understand the proper way of the world. No respect for parents, that one. He should have married one of our own culture."

A single drop of poison. A drop that, unchecked, would seep into their souls.

"Hush now," said Nianzu. "Our son loves and worships his wife, as I worship and love you. It's the proper way. It's the way it should be."

But of course, it wasn't. Ever since their daughter-in-law had lost Nianzu's second unborn grandchild, their son started treating her as though she were made of porcelain. Whatever she said went. Whatever she wanted came. Whatever she didn't want...

Which is why they had to look for a winter home every year.

Nianzu couldn't fathom it. His own name meant "remembering ancestors", and he had devoted his life to that duty. His work had supported his parents until they died; and Mei, his own sweet plum of a wife, had raised their son to follow his example.

And yet they were unable to harvest the fruit of old age. They didn't even have a home to call their own.

"I'll start the supper," Mei said.

They had brought everything with them in their ramshackle van: bins of food, their own wok and bamboo steamers, beddings and soap. Although Nianzu knew the family who owned the mansion was rich, he had disabled the electricity meter nonetheless, not wanting to impose on his unknowing hosts any more than they absolutely must.

"Shall we watch a movie while we eat?" Mei's voice penetrated his thoughts.

Nianzu shuddered, remembering. Last year towards the end of their stay, he had switched on the television in the boy's room, not wanting to disturb Mei in the lounge. What he had seen had sullied more than aroused him.

He'd never told her.

"Yes, my dear. If you like."

They were finishing their jelly when a voice barked out, "What the hell are you people doing here?"

Josh cursed his own lack of foresight. He should have made his escape earlier, when he still had access to his car. Except that standing up to his father was not something he was terribly good at. In fact, it wasn't something he had done before today, ever.

Three hours after the showdown, he was still battling Auckland's public transport to get back to the Shore from the airport's Jet Plus terminal, his damned suitcase getting heavier with every changeover. He would have ditched it if it weren't a Christmas present from Zoë. "Next time you take me out on your boat, you will be able to pack something bigger than your tog bag," she had said in the gift card.

Oh well. Those were the good old days. At least now he and Zoë were on speaking terms again. And he was going to host her Volcano Blast party.

He checked his watch. Going on seven pm. Correction, he was going to be late for the Volcano Blast party unless he pulled his finger out.

He looked through the bus window, hoping for a taxi. Nothing. Not a car in sight driving away from the airport. The opposite direction, however, was one gigantic traffic jam. At this hour, the office-to-home rush should have been over. Surely not everybody wanted to get to the airport?

He tuned his iPod to the local radio station.

"...Aren't Auckland's volcanoes all extinct?"

"Correct. Auckland's existing volcanoes are unlikely to become active again, since they all follow a pattern of short eruptions."

"So we have nothing to worry about?"

"We have absolutely nothing to worry about."

"We are talking to a leading seismologist at Auckland University, Professor Alan Quentin. Tell us, Professor, what about the possibility of new volcanoes appearing in Auckland?"

"Ahem. It's unlikely in the foreseeable future."

"The foreseeable future? How far into the future can you foresee?"

"Well... there is no cause for alarm at this stage. We are monitoring the situation. The probability..."

"It's unlikely, we understand. What would the primary hazards from such an 'unlikely' eruption entail?"

"The most serious hazard would be the initial explosion of rock, gas and steam. The hot lava would travel from the vent and affect the nearby region up to several kilometres in radius. Ash and small debris would fall, causing breathing problems..."

"But, of course, we have 'nothing to worry about', right?"

At 7.23 pm, Josh punched in the code for the pedestrian gate.

The inside lights were always on a randomised timer during the family holidays, so he felt no surprise to find the entertainment area lit up. The hum of the TV in the lounge, though, stopped him from racing upstairs to take a shower.

Josh counted the steps. Five, six, eleven...

His gaze stumbled over two old Asian geezers sitting on his parents' sofa with bowls of something sticky green.

He felt no anger, only astonishment. "What the hell are you people doing here?"

Two faces, wiped clean of all expression, turned to him.

"Me no English," said the old man.

Of course not. Damn the lenient immigration laws.

At 7.31 Josh pointed his finger. "You," he said. "In my," he pointed at himself then gestured a wide all-encompassing circle, "house."

The two old faces remained blank.

Rage rose hot from Nianzu's gall bladder, burned in his belly, constricted his windpipe. This – this *boy* – had the

127

nerve to claim the house as his possession. The house belonged to the man of the family, to the rich white man who made the money by his own sweat and blood... Though perhaps in the case of the white man it had been more brains than sweat or blood.

Mei's soft calming fingers cuddled his own.

"Let it go," she murmured. "This is not the house. This is not our son."

The language of his youth fell softly on his soul, but it could not contain the damage.

"Three year ago I come to this country," he hissed at the boy. "I bring money. Plenty. All my life-money. It buy house in Auckland, that money, good house."

"Ah, so now you not no-English, yes?" teased the boy.

Nianzu froze with humiliation. Impudence was not something he tolerated.

"You quiet. You young. I old. You listen."

To Nianzu's surprise, the boy obeyed.

"I'm sorry. What were you saying about your house?"

"My son and his wife live in house. I live in shack. The money is mine. The name on papers is mine. But I live in shack in garden. I have house, and I don't have house."

"Your daughter in law refuses to have you in the house?"

The old man nodded.

"Wow! The worst I've done was refuse to take a family holiday."

As soon as the words were out of his mouth, Josh realised it would have been better to leave that unsaid.

He continued quickly, "And you've been breaking into our house in the winter when the shack gets too cold?"

The nod was only in the eyes this time.

Josh imagined what his father would have felt if he knew. His precious house with individually picked artwork

128

and hand-woven carpets and imported furniture, turned into a home for the homeless. A fine piece of charity, better than all the balls his parents attended. Except that wouldn't be the way his father saw it.

"I'm sorry," he said. "My friends will be here any minute and I need to change my clothes."

The old man nodded but remained seated alongside his wife.

"Do you understand? I'm having a party."

"You like Mei cook dinner for guests?"

"No!" Josh felt his face grow hot. What kind of a person did this man think he was?

Oh. The kind who runs off from his family and wants to throw two homeless grandparents out of a house that isn't even his, just because he has a party on. "No, thank you."

Seriously though, what was he to do now? Zoë and the gang would be here in twenty minutes, and there he was, old sweat drying under his armpits and two Asians at his table.

"I'm going to take a shower. Excuse me."

Perhaps they would get the hint. Perhaps, when he returned downstairs, they would be gone.

His conscience whispered, "Gone where?"

He didn't care... much.

Nianzu smiled at his wife, a sad smile, a resigned smile. "Go prepare our room. We will watch television there."

Mei's still mouth said volumes.

"I know, my sweetmeat. But there is nothing else to do."

He didn't mean the television, and he knew Mei knew it.

Josh ran down the winding staircase. It was 7.58.

Fresh shirt? Tick.

Aftershave? Tick.

Hair all mussed up from either sleep or sex? Tick.

Protection? He patted the jeans pocket containing three flavoured condoms. Tick.

The old geezers gone? Bugger. Still on the sofa, hand in hand.

"Um. If you guys could, er… go somewhere?"

Nothing.

"Just find a quiet room. The party will be on the wild side, you know. Loud. Crowded."

Come to think of it, the old man was probably used to noisy and crowded back wherever he came from.

Only when the couple shuffled out of the lounge, did Josh allow his breath to escape his throat in a sigh that went on forever.

His watch said 8.02. He slotted ten CDs into the music system and turned up the volume. Set the popcorn popper, checked the coffee machine, threw open the door to the liquor cabinet. The pantry shelves held too few packets of chips, but he did the best he could making up the deficiency with pretzels. Out of peanuts? Bugger.

It was 8.10. Where was Zoë?

He checked his watch again. 8.12.

Now 8.13.

A tremor shook the house. Or was it only his body trembling with uncertainty?

8.25. His mobile vibrated on his hip.

"We're at the gate, but the buzzer's broke," said Zoë.

"Come on in," Josh pressed one of the remote-control buttons.

"No doing. The gate's not moving."

The tremor must have damaged the gate's delicate sliding mechanism. Josh ground a swear word between his teeth and pressed another button. "Try the small gate."

The incessant boom-ba-boom-boom made Nianzu's eyeballs hurt. That was Western music for you. Harsh and monotonous, with no melodic alto of the ruan[3] or caressing of the banhu[4].

The words were impossible to follow, even though the singer repeated every phrase three or four times. It all sounded like a lot of swearing. But then, English was difficult to follow at the best of times.

Sleep was impossible, so he sat with Mei staring at the flickering television screen. Palm trees, blue water, white sand. So beautiful. So unlike Auckland.

Of all the Pacific islands, they had to end up on this one, with its grey cold beaches, he thought.

A shudder surged through the house, the floor vibrated and the television set took a bow to the left before it righted itself.

Nianzu recited a silent apology to the house spirits he had offended with his thoughts. He should have been more grateful, so they were right to get angry. New Zealand was a land of opportunity. His son, and his son's sons, will have jobs in big air-conditioned offices with free coffee and biscuits and time off at statutory holidays. They will have nice big houses… Houses…

The floor began throbbing out another warning.

No. He would not dwell upon his house.

"Here's another one!" Zoë shouted when the walls shook. She downed her fifth passion fruit vodka (Josh hadn't taken his eyes off her since her arrival) and now she reached for the sixth. "It's a wimp. The previous shake was the one with the balls."

The quiver that followed made her drop her glass.

"I'm sorry," she said, but it wasn't about the glass shards. "Good earthquake. Very impressive. You can lie down now. Down, earthquake."

---

[3] A traditional Chinese plucked string instrument
[4] A traditional Chinese bowed string instrument

The music blared out its inane lyrics, something about dropping your ass to the floor. That's what you should do in an earthquake, wasn't it? Drop down?

Josh cupped Zoë's elbow. It was the first time he had touched her this year. Despite everything, past and present, the effect was electrifying.

"You should also lie down," he murmured. "Let me find you a bed."

Her unsteady eyes sought his. "Yes. A bed. With you."

Josh hesitated. Zoë's step was too unsteady to lead her upstairs. He pushed the door to the spare room.

"Oh, hello," she said when she noticed the two old geezers.

Damn it. He had completely forgotten.

The old man needed no explanation.

"Caterers. We cook dinner. Party, yes?" He signalled to his wife and left.

Zoë collapsed onto the bed.

"Come here, you." She patted the space next to her.

"Why suddenly? Why now?"

"Because I'm drunk and I don't give a rat's arse about the past. I've missed you. And I won't even remember any of it in the morning. Nothing to lose."

Josh backed out of the room, knowing that he was going to regret his decision, regretting it already.

"Sleep well, Zoë," he said.

In the kitchen, the old woman's hand whirred as she chopped onions and cabbage into identical narrow strips. When she was done, the old man took over, frying and seasoning and creating miniature parcels of finger food, while the woman carried the platters to the guests.

"Thank you," Josh shouted to make sure they heard him above the music.

"Eat."

He ate. Delicious. It didn't make him feel any better about Zoë.

"No worry. She fine girl. She and you happy. Soon."

The power went out a few seconds before another tremor jiggled the house.

The powdery clang of shattering glass filled the silence. It sounded infinitely better than the music it had replaced.

Nianzu felt disoriented in the blackness. He couldn't remember where the hostess kept the matches, if indeed she even owned a box. The teenagers around him were useless. He heard a lot of swearing (he was certain this time that it was swearing) and still nobody produced a light.

"Mobile phones," he shouted. His ears, made of cotton wool by hours of cacophony, rang and echoed with his own words. "They light like torches!"

All around the room, blue squares of light illuminated frightened faces.

"The earthquake must have knocked down the power station or one of the lines," the boy of the house said. "I'll report the outage… Shit, the 0800 number is out too."

"Engaged?" one of his friends asked.

"No, it sounds like there is a fault on the line."

In the suddenly silent room, the rapid bip-bip-bip of the signal rang like an alarm.

"Car radio," said Nianzu. Honestly, had these youngsters never had to deal with an emergency? "Listen news. And find candles."

"Um, look in the pantry," the boy suggested, his brows drawn together, his gaze already on the interconnecting door that led to the garage.

"Josh!" someone yelled after him. "What about the matches?"

"The cigar room, second door to the left!"

The boy's name was Josh. Nianzu wondered what the name meant. Names were important that way, they influenced the owner's destiny. His own son's name was Bao. Treasure. No matter what Bao had done or would do in the future, he would always remain his parents' treasure. Precious. Hard. Cold. And unattainable.

Candle flames dotted the large entertainment area. Mei had brought the large mirror from the hallway and placed it alongside the flames to amplify them.

Josh entered the flickering circle of light. "The Shore, all the way to Warkworth, is without electricity," he announced. His voice wobbled. "Many roads have been damaged by the quake, so nobody knows how long it'll take for the power lines to be restored. People are urged to stay indoors and to take precautions."

So much upheaval over a common earthquake, Nianzu thought. *The earthquakes of his childhood, those were earthquakes. But then*, he conceded, *the meagre food tasted better in those days and the air smelled fresher even though it was polluted. Your past is always a fairytale, your own personal fairytale you tell yourself whenever life weighs you down.*

"I don't know what precautions," Josh replied. "Stay under a table or in a door-frame?"

"How long? How long before we can go home?"

"Man, I don't know. Give your folks a call to see if they're all right. Tell them you're all right. You can all camp out here until the situation stabilises."

"Josh?" Zoë's voice joined the others. "There is no water. I was taking a shower…"

"The water is gas-heated," he interrupted. He didn't need images of Zoë taking a shower. "It should be all ri…"

"No. I mean there is no water, full stop." She sounded completely sober. And scared.

"Shit!"

"We use swimming pool for water," said the old man. "Buckets for toilet."

Josh wondered where the hell his parents stored the buckets. It was the only house he'd ever lived in, apart from hotel resorts and their own various holiday houses, but he had no clue about things like buckets. The old woman, meanwhile, had already brought some in from the outside. The laundry room? The garden shed? Josh had no idea. He grabbed hold of two buckets and headed towards the pool.

Zoë followed him.

"Look at all the stars," she said. "I didn't know we had so many. And the moon is almost full. Pretty."

It was a good moment, to stand under the stars with the girl of your dreams.

"Do you think a volcano might…" she broke off.

"I sure hope so," he lied. "It'll be spectacular. They say when Rangitoto was being born, you could watch it for years, and the sky was all red. Must have been awesome."

Her eyes sought his in the moonlight.

"What did we fight about? I can't even remember anymore."

Josh could tell her. He remembered every sound, every gesticulation. "Let's not go there," he said. "Friends again?"

"More than that, I should hope."

His lips were on hers and Josh didn't know whether he had moved first or Zoë, just that she tasted of salt and warmth. He knotted his fingers in her hair, his whole body clenched in anticipation.

"Where is that water?" Josh recognised Zach, Zoë's twin brother, his voice so similar to hers. "You guys drowned or gone skinny-dipping? Jesus! Can't see a bloody thing out here."

Josh almost cried out in frustration. To get so close to the action and not follow through *twice* in less than an hour was twice too much.

"We're almost done. Just have to uncover the pool. Go back inside."

Another silhouette materialised in the darkness.

"No uncover," said the old man. "If volcano come, ash bad for water."

"If volcano come, we all dead," mocked Zach.

Most likely, thought Nianzu. The rivers of molten lava, rocks flying all over the place, the hot blasts of poisonous gases…

Aloud he said, "No, no, no. Small volcano okay. Just keep pool cover."

They would also need dust masks to breathe the air polluted by the eruption. And goggles to protect the eyes from the ash fall and from the acid rain. He double-checked the roof – its triangular shape would slow down ash accumulation, so they wouldn't be buried alive. Not that Auckland volcanoes made so much ash you needed to worry about it.

These teenagers here were helpless in an emergency. Fortunately he and Mei had come prepared. The food they had brought, combined with the non-perishables in the pantry, should suffice for a few weeks. There were enough gas bottles in the storeroom to heat up many barbecues, and the sea that began where the garden ended would provide the meat. And if the motorboat's petrol ran out, there would always be seagulls. They tasted disgusting, but he and Mei had eaten worse. Nothing compared to the plastic hamburgers and chemical-laden fries that these poor rich children were used to, but bad enough.

Mei was waiting for him when he returned inside.

"I spoke to Bao. They are all fine. Enough candles and food."

"Water?"

"They filled the bath as soon as the first earthquake came."

Nianzu nodded approval.

"Did you tell him to pour the water into the toilet tank to flush normally?"

"Yes. He says to thank you. They didn't think of that. They would have used the bucket straight."

A small victory. In his old age, he could still be useful.

"Did he…" Nianzu couldn't find the words.

"He didn't ask us to go back."

Zoë's phone rang. She glanced at the Caller ID.

"It's my mum."

"Aren't you going to answer?"

"Nah."

Josh squeezed her hand. He would have ignored a call from his parents too. Not that they bothered to contact him since he had stormed out of the jet terminal at the airport. Not once.

His wonderful superhero dad. When had he turned into a rich fart who didn't know about real life? This Asian geezer, for example, could cook, break into a house without setting off security alarms, handle a power outage and make provisions in case of ash fall. All his father knew about emergency situations was how to avoid them. His father ran away from his own native South Africa when the political situation threatened to shake his lifestyle, and now from Josh's native New Zealand when nature threatened a similar shake up. The Asian guy hadn't run away from his country of birth: he ran towards better prospects in the country of his choice. Therein lay the difference.

"Josh? I'm scared."

137

Zoë's hand was still in his, warm and soft and quivering.

He wanted to tell her there was nothing to worry about. He wanted to promise to keep her safe. But all he did was raise her small fist to his lips, the old-fashioned way.

"Jesus, Josh, now you're scaring her."

"Piss off, Zach."

Zoë's twin sniggered. "Where to? Mum says both bridges to The Shore are inaccessible. Collapsed or something. It's not on the news but she and Dad tried to drive across and it's all barricaded."

Josh felt Zoë's whole body go rigid. "Why did they try? How did they know we were here? Zach, you are a dead man."

"They have the right, Zo. Jesus! Imagine how they worried. They phoned you like a million times and you never picked up!"

"Whatever."

"Mister Josh. Please. You come see."

"What is it?" Josh didn't feel like letting go of Zoë's hand.

"You come see."

"I'll go with you, Josh." Zoë got up to her feet, her fingers interlacing with his. "It's eerie inside with all those candles. Like a funeral."

Outside, the swimming pool's cover was peeled back in one corner. Josh expected the moonlight to fall onto a glossy triangle of shimmering silver. But the triangle was black.

"The water…" Josh trailed off in disbelief.

"Going away," said the old man. "Earthquake crack pool."

"Tell us what we can do."

Nianzu's ribcage was tight. Here – finally – was the appreciation he had never received from his own son.

"English radio no want panic. But Chinese radio say good idea evacuate Shore."

The girl's voice, when she spoke, was hoarse. "The roads are inaccessible. The bridge is gone. We are stuck here."

A cloud extinguished the moon at that moment, as if to add significance to the words.

Nianzu bit back his answer. Waited. This was Josh's chance.

"No problem, Zoë. Leave it all to me," said the boy. "I'll take the motorboat over to the marina to fetch the big boat, then I'll come back for you all."

Well done, thought Nianzu. *Act like a man, get the girl. Forever, not just for a night.*

"Where will we go, Josh?" Zoë asked. "Where will we evacuate to?"

"The big boat has desalination facilities, so it could serve as a base if needed. Sometimes it's not important where to run to. Sometimes the important thing is, where you're running from."

Nianzu was impressed. That was a good piece of philosophy for a teenager. Though in reality, somewhere in mainland Auckland would probably do fine as a destination for their purposes.

He felt a hand on his shoulder.

"Will you organise packing the supplies while I'm gone?" Josh asked.

"Yes."

"And look after Zoë for me? I have to leave her here. The motorboat is not safe for her if the volcano…"

"Zoë. So-Yi. A gift of long life. No need worry. You two long life with many grandchildren. Now go."

Josh laughed.

"Phone your son too. Tell him to get ready. You don't want to leave without him, do you?"

139

Nianzu shook his head even though he was quite sure the gesture would be invisible in the dark. His soul felt like ice.

"My son's wife, she no go."

Josh's tone was confident, smug almost. "If I peg your daughter-in-law right, she will change her mind as soon as she sees my – my father's – boat with its on-deck swimming pool and sauna. You will be her best friend yet."

Nianzu was sure Josh pegged Bao's wife exactly right.

Winter Wine

New York, 28 May

@TinaTweets: Ashton invited me to New Zealand for a month. Our summer, their winter. Thoughts? **#isthislove**

@LivvyOnLife: Yes!!! At last! **#thismustbelove** Actually - no!!! Too early. You need time to process the past - **#reboundsucks**. Then again - maybe?

@TinaTweets: Confused much, LOL? I'm done processing. Dealt with being dumped. Ready for **#adventure**. Haven't seen Ashton since we were 12. **#firstcrush**

@LivvyOnLife: But their winter? You want to give up our famous New York heat waves for snowstorms like those in Lord of the Rings?

@TinaTweets: I'll pack my scarf. So excited! Totally ready to make love and summer wine!

@LivvyOnLife: Winter wine, more like it. What is your **#winterwine** made of?

@TinaTweets: Ashton's kisses, of course. Two weeks to go and counting! **#nzmustdo**

Auckland, 10 June

@TinaTweets: Landed safely. Ashton meeting me at the airport. After 30 hours of travel, I need a shower and makeup.

@LivvyOnLife: You're procrastinating. Perfume, lipstick, then go through customs and meet the man of your dreams!

@TinaTweets: Livvy, I'm scared.

@LivvyOnLife: Go.

Auckland, 11 June

@TinaTweets: Auckland is gorgeous! Volcano cones in vivid green, slate grey of sea waves, Sky Tower reigns like a rocket over the city.

@LivvyOnLife: Stuff Auckland. Tell me about Ashton. **#isthislove**

@TinaTweets: I am telling you about Ashton. Rockets, volcanoes, waves. Get it?

@LivvyOnLife: Wait, what? Pull your mind out of the gutter! And – you didn't, did you? The first night? Tina!

@TinaTweets: Kidding. Separate motel rooms. Ashton is a perfect gentleman. I wish he wasn't, though! Liv, he's every bit as smart and funny as online...

@TinaTweets: ...and much better looking than at school. His photos don't do him justice. Also, he has a Kiwi accent now. Mega cute.

Rotorua, 14 June

@LivvyOnLife: Earth to Tina.

@TinaTweets: Sorry. So much to tell you. Too much.

@LivvyOnLife: !!! ☺☺ ☺ ???

@TinaTweets: No, nothing like that. I mean, we're very cuddly all the time, but still separate rooms. I think I like that.

@LivvyOnLife: You're after a man with a slow hand?

@TinaTweets: Exactly. Anyway, saw Hobbiton at last. Got close and personal to hobbit burrows. Also, took a boat ride through some caves with a funny name and lots of glow worms.

@LivvyOnLife: **#romantic**

@TinaTweets: You have no idea. **#romantic #dreamy #notsteamyyet**

Rotorua, 15 June

@TinaTweets: Long soaks in natural hot springs with the guy who might just be The One...

@TinaTweets: ...Mock mud fights in geothermal mud pools...

@TinaTweets: ...Life is good.

@LivvyOnLife: **#winterwine**?

@TinaTweets: You bet.

Napier, 17 June

@TinaTweets: Love Napier's Art Deco architecture. Sad to learn it's the result of tragedy - 1931 earthquake, at least 256 people died...

@TinaTweets: ...Pensive today. Life is short...

@TinaTweets: ...Carpe diem. Right?

@LivvyOnLife: Um. Yes in principle. But what are you actually asking?

@TinaTweets: Feels like I've been given an opportunity with this trip – to do something different with my time. Something worthwhile. What do you think?

@LivvyOnLife: I think time is a funny thing. You say it's the 17th. Still the 16th back home. So did you lose a day? Did we?...

@LivvyOnLife: ...But what's the opportunity you mentioned? I googled Napier and it's definitely rebuilt, so it can't be that? **#TinaWantsToChangeTheWorld**

@TinaTweets: Later. Our tour bus awaits. We're visiting five wine estates today. **#winterwine**

@TinaTweets: PS Yeah. Tina definitely wants to change the world.

Napier, 17 June

@TinaTweets: Thank goodness for the door-to-door service on the wine tour. Ashton is a superb driver but we've had a lot of wine. Bed now. **#NZwinerocks**

@LivvyOnLife: Bed? What do you mean? As in together? One bed?

@LivvyOnLife: Tina?

Napier, 18 June

@TinaTweets: Headache. A tiny one. **#winterwine** Well worth it...

@TinaTweets: ...One of the wines we've tasted grows on an old riverbed which diverted its course during the flood in the 1860s...

@LivvyOnLife: Fascinating. So? What happened after "bed now"?

@TinaTweets: We went to bed.

@LivvyOnLife: OMG! The same bed?

@TinaTweets: The same.

@LivvyOnLife: Tell.

@TinaTweets: We fell asleep straight away. Too much wine. But hey, at least we slept together…

@TinaTweets: …Also, this morning Ashton picked me up fireman-style and started running around the room. When I asked him why, he said…

@TinaTweets: …"I want to make sure I can save you in case there's another earthquake."

Palmerston North, 19 June

@TinaTweets: Absolutely nothing to do in this town. Will try to seduce Ashton tonight.

@LivvyOnLife: What about the slow hand thought?

@TinaTweets: It's plenty slow. Any tips on how to seduce a guy who's already into you but wants to give you time to shed your emotional baggage?

@LivvyOnLife: Wine?

@TinaTweets: Been there, done that, and the T-shirt doesn't fit. ☺

@LivvyOnLife: Google says: tease, talk dirty, write dirty, surprise him, show up naked (bring beer), suggest something new.

@TinaTweets: Like, let's do more than kiss? **#melting #hesureknowshowtokiss**

@LivvyOnLife: How about telling him you've shed your emotional baggage?

Wellington, 20 June

@TinaTweets: This is indeed the cutest capital city ever. Ashton is friends with an ice cream shop owner, so we made chocolate ice cream. **#oompaloompas**

@LivvyOnLife: I take it nothing happened in Palmerston North?

@TinaTweets: Nothing ever happens in Palmerston North. No, that's not true. We did play never-have-I-ever.

@LivvyOnLife: And?

@TinaTweets: And now I truly know him. **#ithinkthisislove**

Wellington, 21 June

@TinaTweets: Tonight is the longest night of the year. Ashton asked me to pack an overnight bag – we'll leave the suitcases in the car. **#adventure**

Ferry to Picton, 23 June

@TinaTweets: The longest night of the year felt surprisingly short, even though we didn't sleep a wink. #thisislove #heistheone

@LivvyOnLife: Dare I hope you've finally done the deed? Danced the horizontal tango? Rode the broomstick?

@TinaTweets: To heaven and back, girlfriend.

@LivvyOnLife: Phew! I might actually need a cigarette. Now, all the details, quick.

@TinaTweets: Not all the details. But the PG-rated ones include: helicopter ride, secluded lodge, outdoor bubble bath, views of...

@TinaTweets: ...snow-capped mountains, craggy coastline, dolphins playing in the shipping lane. We may have heard wild horses...

@TinaTweets: ...The Pinot Noir was from a region called Glistening Waters. Tasted of maraschino cherries and vanilla. The best ever **#winterwine**...

@TinaTweets: ...Anyway, we're crossing the Cook Strait and we have a private cabin on the ferry. Double bed. Bye! Definitely won't BRB![5]

Picton, 24 June

@TinaTweets: Wine tasting in an underground cellar – legendary! We're on a honey farm now. When I grow up, I want to be a beekeeper.

Greymouth, 26 June

@TinaTweets: Coastal rocks shaped like stacks of pancakes. Who would have thought? **#nzscenery** #bucketlist

Franz Josef Glacier, 27 June

@TinaTweets: **#speechless**

Nelson, 28 June

@TinaTweets: We're home. Ashton has – actually has – a teeny vineyard. And beehives. And sheep. **#inlove**

---

[5] Be Right Back (online jargon)

@LivvyOnLife: Wait. Are you in love with the guy or with his new country?

@TinaTweets: Ashton. He completes me. We laugh and get lost in conversations for hours.

Nelson, 30 June

@TinaTweets: Ashton asked me to stay in NZ.

@LivvyOnLife: Tina! If you tell me you didn't say yes...

@TinaTweets: I said: "What took you so long?"

Eva, Evita, Eva

Eva – Argentina, 1947

My name is Eva Anna Paula Braun.

Who am I? I wear many masks. I'm not defined by the man who was my lover, even though you've probably only heard of me in connection with him. And yet I'm a force that changed the course of international events and made the post-war world what it has become.

I've been inspired to put pen to paper because of something Hermann Göring, the once commander-in-chief of the Luftwaffe, declared during his recent trial in Nuremberg: "The victor will always be the judge, and the vanquished the accused." Göring was judged by the victors and sentenced to death. He escaped hanging by swallowing the cyanide capsule I smuggled to him. It was a kinder end for a soldier who had done his duty, obeyed the laws of his country, and fought honourably for his Fatherland and his people.

Germany is quelled for now, though I have no doubt we shall rise again. Meanwhile, the winners are sculpting the narrative in which they are the heroes and we are the butchers, as though Joseph Stalin didn't kill as many – if not more. And that's not the only lie making its way into the post-war world wearing the mask of gospel truth.

Almost anything you have heard about me in the news and from the gossip mill is false. You know me as Adolf Hitler's mistress – that bit is true. Per my birth certificate, I was born on 6 February 1912 – also true. You probably believe I died on 30 April 1945 – that's not true, obviously.

My story began sixteen years prior to my supposed suicide in the Führerbunker, the day I met Adolf Hitler and put on the mask of a woman smitten with love. He must have sensed that we were alike as soon as he laid his eyes on me in Heinrich Hoffman's photography workshop back in 1929.

It was a miserable October day, the golden touch of summer long forgotten, the magic of snow still to come. I was standing on a ladder, restocking the chemicals, when I heard the jangle of the door as it swung open. Herr Hoffman and the visitor exchanged greetings. Then silence.

I put down the jar of sodium thiosulfate, which we used in the darkroom as a fixer, and turned my head, well aware of how that small shift in neck and shoulders changed the lines of my body to my advantage. A small-statured dark-moustached gentleman was gaping at me. His wasn't the first slack jaw I've encountered, for the shape of my legs seems to have this effect on most men, but it's the first time the intensity of a male gaze was so thick you could stab it with a dessert fork and eat it like a triangle of Prinzregententorte.

I liked that look enough to string Adolf along for years to come. My hips know how to sway just so, my eyes know how to promise heaven, and my brain knows seductive words that make men feel like emperors of the universe. Most importantly, I understand the power of delayed gratification.

Before I agreed to a kiss, and a chaste one at that, Adolf Hitler moved me into a private apartment and confirmed me in the role of his personal photographer. Whenever I sensed his infatuation with me wane, I allowed him another graze in my virginal armour; and when he grew bored with my body, I let him believe he could invade my soul – I even staged a suicide attempt to convince him how badly I craved his attention. I played cat and mouse with him, I groomed him, wrote his speeches, and stroked his ego. Was I responsible for his party's stellar rise? I like to think so.

German intellectuals were shocked when Hitler won the

elections. He was a boisterous clown, they claimed, his propaganda crude, his rallies tacky, his philosophy simplistic. What they didn't understand was that Hitler kept delivering the very message the masses wanted to hear. Sometimes that's enough to be crowned king.

Let me say it again: I wrote his speeches.

Overnight, my position as Hitler's woman became both extremely powerful and fraught with peril. It was safer for me to pretend that I had no sway with the Führer, so we kept separate bedrooms and I seldom accompanied him on official business. I also made every effort to present myself as foolish, frivolous and – most importantly – inconsequential. His closest advisers swore that my only interests were fashion and film, and that my poor little head would explode if it ever tried to fill itself with politics. Dolfi and I laughed about that every night, me sipping French wine, him with a goblet of what he referred to as his *youth elixir* made of bull testicles and bear liver.

The problem though? Adolf Hitler was not very smart. Cunning – yes; charismatic -yes, yet not strategic enough to win a world war. He stretched his armies in Greece, ordered inferior tanks to be manufactured for the Eastern Front, and devoted far too much energy to amassing a personal fortune in works of fine art and gold. I am grateful, of course. His collection is serving us well, me and my daughter, and the man I call my husband.

Most analysts agree that Stalingrad was the beginning of the end for the Third Reich, and they're right. Only time will tell whether historians will ever find out about Adolf Hitler's personal cypher machine, the Lorenz, and my inadvertent role in its failure. The date was 30 August 1941. Dolfi and I were paying Greece a semi-incognito visit, ostensibly to assess the conquered territory, although it was just an opportunity for him to relax and paint a few Greek landscapes in shades of blue and green oils.

It was there, at the German Army High Command in Athens, that I first noticed Lothar. I had entered the bureau with a long letter from the Führer to his propaganda minister, Paul Joseph Goebbels, who was stationed in Vienna at the time. The letter needed encrypting, and when I handed it over to the cypher machine's operator, my first thought was that Dolfi had planned to play a prank on me, for the cypher machine's operator looked exactly like him – minus the signature facial hair.

Straight off, I recognised the value of my discovery. I had found the Führer's double! Good enough for official outings, for waving to crowds and even for short speeches with his voice distorted through the loudspeaker. I lingered, observing the operator as he worked, marvelling at how perfect he would be as soon as he'd grown a moustache.

My presence must have been distracting, for the operator made a mistake when sending the original letter, then blundered even worse by resending a shortened version using the same key. I didn't know it at the time, of course, and he only shared his theory on our long trip to Argentina four years later: he suspected that his actions on the day we'd met could have enabled the enemy to break the Lorenz code. He is an intelligent man, Lothar, with a passion for cypher and mathematics. And for me. His greatest passion is me.

But I digress. Back in 1941, Lothar returned with us to Berlin and assumed his duties of impersonating the Führer at official functions, while Dolfi and I spent the evenings home alone. Soon all those intimate evenings by the fire resulted in my belly bulging despite the fact that I had trouble holding down food. As much as I hate to admit it, when I learnt that I was pregnant, I resented the parasite who had lodged itself inside me and was nourishing itself with my very body. It was only when baby Eva slipped out of me after a night of agony, that I realised I would do anything to secure her safety and happiness.

Unfortunately, foregoing public appearances also freed up Adolf's time to design and mount his disastrous campaign on Russia. Although he spent a lot more hours on strategizing Operation Barbarossa than he ever did in my bed, the results were not nearly as fruitful. By 1943, it was clear that we were on an almost-certain trajectory to lose the war. My informants carried whispers that Heinrich Himmler was liquidating his assets and steering the money to secret bank accounts in South America. His plan, rumour had it, was to set up a Fourth Reich somewhere outside of Europe.

The idea was not without merit. While I cared not to replicate the Reich anywhere or any-when, I judged Himmler's financial manoeuvres sagacious enough to follow suit. After all, I had a daughter and her future to worry about.

And worry I did, because of the asinine Nazi notion that an honourable death was better than defeat. Almost everybody who was anybody in the Party purchased convenient capsules of cyanide – copious amounts, sufficient to poison entire households. Our family was no exception.

"Would you really do it, if the time came?" I asked Adolf one morning. I was eating a thick slice of ham on my sourdough, although by then he would hardly touch meat, contenting himself with oatmeal for breakfast.

"Naturally." A single word, so full of conviction, it punched me straight in the heart.

"What about…" I couldn't bring myself to say her name. It would be like a curse, a verdict clinching her fate. "What about our daughter?"

"I'd crush the capsule myself and pour it down her throat." No emotion in his voice. I've seen him more agitated over a fly in the dining room.

That was the precise moment in which I started to hate him. And yet when he turned his gaze to me, question marks in his eyes, his words seeking confirmation that I'd swallow poison for him, I got out of my seat and hugged him. Pressing his head into my breasts so that he wouldn't see my expression while I moulded my face once again into a mask of adoration, I replied, "Do you think I would let you die alone, my treasure? I will stay with you until the end."

I kept my promise. I stayed with him to the end, indeed. His end. On the last day of April 1945, I walked with him to the bunker, having made sure that enough people witnessed our death march. Once we were alone, I offered him the capsule, and when he recoiled from it, I shot him in the head.

It would have been better not to burn his body, to leave it there for the Soviets to find and identify, but I had no choice. The female corpse that I had procured on the streets of Berlin didn't resemble me much, so I dressed it in my favourite frock, pressed a goodbye note in my handwriting into its fist, and let flames of living fire become the perfect makeup artist for the dead.

It worked out well, as it turned out, for many of the German ruling party survivors assumed that it had to be Hitler's double who had died in that bunker, and the Führer was the one who had escaped in the U-boat with little Eva and me and my two Scottish terriers.

Hitler's German Shepherd, Blondi, had been fed the poisoned pill by his master moments before the cowardly ruler escaped into that concrete reinforced bunker. Fortunately, the sodium thiosulfate we used to utilise in the photography shop is an excellent antidote for cyanide. I had it at the ready and Blondi survived, though I didn't love him enough to take him to Argentina with us. The space in the submarine was precious, literally worth its volume in gold, so I sent Blondi to my sister as a farewell gift. We weren't particularly close, my sister and I, so she assumed the dog was mine, and – in her mind – it only reinforced the story of my suicide.

The journey to Argentina was dreadful. Hot, stale air. Tinned food. The longest possible walk: about two hundred feet in one direction in theory, but with all the crates of paintings and jewellery, there was no space to move at all. Crippling fear of being detected. And shot at. And yet, the hardest to take, was the constant weight of defeat. I don't know how I would have coped without Lothar. He was my rock, my happy place, the polar opposite of Herr Hitler.

After months under the sea, we landed in Mar del Plata, an Argentinian resort south and east of Buenos Aires. It felt like heaven to take a bath, eat fresh fruit, and feel safe. At first, we stayed in the casino's luxurious hotel, but it meant wearing disguising masks, whenever we ventured out of our suite so last year we moved to our new home. It's the most lavish of all the mansions in the freshly built secure complex that boasts a sports centre, a movie theatre and even a school. Our neighbours are fellow Germans who believe that Lothar is their beloved Führer. They're ready to regroup, waiting for him to give the word and reveal his new plan. Let them wait. And should they ever get impatient or suspicious, I still have the trusted Walther 7.65 with which I shot Adolf Hitler.

I've made acquaintances outside our German community too. The Argentinian president is an intriguing man, even if his ideals are somewhat at odds with my beliefs. His new wife is lovely. Utterly lovely. Her name is also Eva, though her people call her Evita.

Argentina is picturesque, and having measured east and west, I'm grateful for my new life here. Lothar's love for me is so vast, it encompasses little Eva as though she were his own daughter. I'm grateful for that, and I'm grateful that my daughter is her own person, with no bits that remind me of her biological beginnings.

And yet, I miss my homeland. On nights without a cloud, the Argentinian sky looks like my widest diamond tiara, and some German constellations shine for me even in this distant place on the other side of the equator. On those nights, the stars sing the song of my fatherland, the thing of the past. If I could interpret their patterns, what would they tell me about the future?

Dallas, 1963

My name is Eva Marie Perón, née Duarte. Perhaps you know me as Evita and think I died of cancer eleven years ago. This story will put it right.

Who am I? An illegitimate daughter, a child prostitute, a saint, a socialist, a fascist, a feminist. Of all those labels, only the first one is correct: I'm female, and my parents never married, as my father already had a lawful family up the road. I grew up poor, yet that made me neither a courtesan nor a collectivist.

My husband's government has been compared to Franco's Spain and Mussolini's Italy, yet while his policies could be considered fascism (albeit fascism that favoured the working class), I had zero interest in politics. True, I advocated for the women's right to vote and to be elected to government positions – yet it had nothing to do with a political stance, it was all self-interest. Because of Argentina's traditionalistic values, it was considered revolutionary of me to appear alongside my husband in a political campaign, or to voice my opinions. And so, to be contrary, I voiced many opinions on workers' rights, women's rights and the abject poverty of my fellow countrymen.

An unforeseen (yet nevertheless welcome) consequence of my stance was that it raised my public profile on the international stage. In 1946, just a few months after my husband became the President of Argentina, the US media bestowed on me the label of the "most powerful, shrewd and hard-working member of his cabinet". For five years, North America dubbed me the exemplar modern woman, destined for vice-presidency or even to take over as President from my much older husband when the time came.

The time never came. Instead, the Cold War intensified, which led to an almost-fanatical propaganda in the USA: my husband's leftist government was branded communist, while feminism turned into an undesirable. The USA propaganda shifting towards women's domesticity meant that throughout the 1950s I was depicted as a power-hungry abomination, even though in my native Argentina I remained the sweetheart, the mother of the nation, the patron of the poor – perhaps largely because they believed me dead.

But allow me to backtrack. The year 1945 was a big one – for most of the world, and especially for me. Yes, it was the year the second war had ended. It was also the year I married Juan Perón and gave birth to his son (though in reverse order). Most importantly – for the purpose of this story, at least – it was the year I met Eva Braun.

Although history portrays her as a monster and me as a martyr, she's my soulmate in every respect. We both come from nothing, and yet we both discovered how to use our womanly wiles to become First Ladies of our respective fatherlands. Our children were kept a secret from the world for political reasons, although – to be fair – Adolf Hitler had known about his daughter, while I chose not to inform my staunchly Catholic husband that I had borne him an heir out of wedlock.

157

Eva Braun's de facto husband is reviled for being the blueprint Nazi. My legally wedded spouse is a Nazi sympathiser to this day, although he may simply be a Nazi-gold sympathiser. After the war, many a large fortune changed hands whenever a new German family set up residence in Mar del Plata, in a security village known – either ironically or optimistically – as *Heimat*. I know about the Nazi bribes for sure, because my "non-political goodwill" tour of Europe in 1947 was a cover story for an important bank deposit. You know the drill: Switzerland, a secret account, no paper trail leading back to Juan.

To help the European economies recover from the Second World War, and to aid Spain additionally in the aftermath of its civil war, I convinced my husband to send 400,000 tonnes of wheat, 120,000 tonnes of corn, 8,000 tonnes of cooking oil, 10,000 tonnes of lentils, 20,000 tonnes of frozen meat, 5,000 tonnes of cured meat and 50,000 boxes of eggs to the government of General Francisco Franco. Did that unintentionally help prop up his dictatorship in Spain? Perhaps. All I know is that thanks to a very wild and elaborate night I spent in my husband's bed, millions of Spaniards ate dinner, so I'll take it as a win.

I wooed Europe on that tour, dubbed the *Rainbow Tour* because of a silly magazine article that compared me to a rainbow spanning Argentina and the Old World. I got a rosary from Pope Pius XII, a kiss on the cheek from Charles de Gaulle, and a very large blue diamond from the Greek shipping magnate, Aristotle Onassis, who later claimed that he had slept with me on that tour. Please. Five foot nothing, classless and downright rude, he wouldn't be able to have me for all the diamond mines in the world.

As I mentioned before, by 1951 the tide was turning against me. The United States criticised my "personal lifestyle marked by expensive clothes and private jets" as incongruent with the bleeding leftist views I propagated, and they suggested my place should be in the kitchen, not in a Vice President's office. In truth, I was also becoming bored with it all: I'd had my time in the limelight, I'd toured the world, I'd tended to the ill. Juan was seeking to be re-elected, and the stress was becoming too much. I couldn't eat and lost weight, prompting the rumour mill to speculate about my health.

That gave me an idea. If my dearest friend, Eva Braun, could fake her own death, so could I. On 26 July 1952, radio programmes across Argentina got interrupted by the announcement that Eva Peron, Spiritual Leader of the Nation, was dead. A life-size wax figurine, playing the part of my embalmed body, remained on public display for weeks. My people prayed to it and called for my canonisation as a saint, while I walked among the mourners in a thin latex mask that made my features anonymous.

I escaped the trappings of my former life just in time, too. Isolation and high inflation were beginning to ruin my country's economy. When Juan Perón got ousted from the presidency and exiled to Spain, my son and I left Argentina for the shores of North America.

Aristotle Onassis, whom I had met in Monte Carlo during my *Rainbow Tour*, had a lot of useful contacts in the States thanks to his wartime shipping enterprise, and facilitated my relocation, together with all the documents and credentials confirming me a US citizen. On this occasion, I did have sex with him – not, as he supposed, in exchange for the paperwork, but because staying the night at his palatial manor put me in the right place the next day, when I shared the lunch table with the FBI boss, J. Edgar Hoover – a contact that would prove useful many times over.

The only downside of moving Stateside was the heartbreak

caused by parting with my dearest friend. Eva Braun did not want to leave the haven of the security village in Mar del Plata to accompany me to the States. In 1960, however, the noose was beginning to tighten around the former Nazi elite living in Argentina. Adolf Eichmann, the main engineer of the Holocaust, was kidnapped by Israeli commandos in the Buenos Aires suburb where he resided. Fearing for her safety, Eva and her family decided to join me in my new country.

She managed to immigrate thanks to the direct intervention of J. Edgar Hoover: he issued a policy that allowed Eva and other Nazi sympathisers to live under assumed identities (and behind latex masks) right inside the US as potential informants in the Cold War.

This arrangement worked beautifully for several years, until the president found out about it. Even though he hated the Soviets and felt embarrassed by the Bay of Pigs fiasco, John Fitzgerald Kennedy couldn't accept a spy network made up of Hitler's friends, subordinates, and a mistress who was also the mother of Hitler's only child and now married to someone who sure looked like the former ruler of the Third Reich.

Kennedy was going to blow it all up, so you see, I had to act. He was an infamous womaniser, and to this day it hurts me to remember that he had rejected my advances. His high moral ground cost him his life. With FBI's blessing and their extensive dossiers of communist sympathisers, I selected Lee Harvey Oswald as the sacrificial goat, the patsy, the pawn that slays the king.

Pretending to work for the Soviet Embassy in Mexico, I established contact with Oswald and convinced him to accept the task in exchange for his safe passage to the Soviet Union and a place at the ruling party's table. I planned out the logistics of the assassination. I provided the rifle. Hell, I even seduced Oswald to close the deal – well, all right, it didn't hurt that I was attracted to his Marine Corps past and would have bedded him just for the pleasure of it.

In the end, though, he wasn't the solution he promised to be, so I had to implement a backup option. You see, I was the assassin who had fired shots from the grassy knoll, a small hill inside the Dealey plaza, exactly above Kennedy and to his right during the assassination.

It's almost Christmas, the time for celebration and cheer, the time for friends and families and feasts. My dearest friend Eva is fifty-one, I forty-four. Our children are young adults, and although little Eva is a few years older than my Pedro, I have a feeling their unique and secret past will bind their destinies and they'll end up together, formalising the unofficial ties our families have forged.

If the public were to ever find out about us, the leading conspiracy theory would probably be that Eva Braun and Evita are a romantic couple. Nothing could be further from the truth: Eva is deeply in love with her Lothar, while I – I value my freedom. Freedom from fame and responsibilities. Freedom to run around and try everything new. Freedom to enjoy a man, then leave him in his bed while I return to my unsoiled home – to Pedro, Eva, Little Eva and Lothar.

Speaking of conspiracy theories, Kennedy is barely in his grave, and already the speculations, fantasies and outright lies are spreading like wildfire all over the land. The Mob did it. It was the mysterious man who carried an umbrella on a sunny day. The CIA echelons, led by anti-Castro and anti-communist factions, were somehow involved.

My favourite one is that it was Jack Ruby who drove a gunman to the grassy knoll, although my chauffeur on that occasion was Eva Braun. I didn't know who Jack Ruby was until he killed Oswald, though his motive escapes me for now. Obviously, it was fortuitous for me to have Oswald silenced, but I can promise you that Jack Ruby was not one of my lovers. J. Edgar Hoover, on the other hand…

Have I said too much?

Eva – New Zealand, 2021

My Insta handle is All4TheEnvironmentEva. I was named after two of my great-grandmothers. Historians haven't been kind to them, but I know their true stories, whispered to me by my mother, and her mother's mother before that.

"But Grandma, is that really true?" I would ask her.

And she'd reply, "Those who only tell the truth are not worth listening to."

I'm nothing like the two Evas who came before me. So who am I? I wear many masks. One mask is that of a vegetarian, but that's just what I choose to eat. One mask is that of a computer engineer and a white hat hacker, but that's just what I do. One mask is that of a mother because I have a baby girl, another that of a communist for my beliefs, or a lesbian for fucking women, or a slut for fucking men – many, many men, because that's the fastest and easiest way to get them to do my bidding. And yet those masks don't define me any more than my blonde hair would.

Am I a terrorist or a fighter for a better future? I used to agonize over the answer. Now I know that I'm simply both, depending on whose eyes I look through.

Looking through my own eyes, I see what's become of the world and I just want to puke. The Boomers destroyed the economy and raped the environment – and what does my generation do? Peaceful marches with Covid face masks and saccharine placards, online petitions that achieve sweet FA, TikToks that absolve us of all responsibility for the outcome.

162

Pacifists, all of them. I crave a different kind of buzz. Mother Earth needs terrorists on her side: people who will bomb plastic industries, seal oil wells, ground aeroplanes and frack the living daylights out of fracking companies. Because there is no Planet B, you know.

Eva Braun, one of my great-grandmothers, worried that the generations to come would not know the real her. She was right. *Eva Braun will prove a great disappointment to historians*, one of the Wikipedia entries reads. Ha, ha, bloody ha.

Nobody will say that about me. To quote Winston Churchill, "History will be kind to me for I will write it." And to quote his arch enemy, Adolf Hitler, my great-grandfather: "The victor will never be asked if he told the truth." I intend to be victorious.

Who am I? My name is Eva. I'm a woman. I'm dangerous. And I get shit done.

Watch this space. The next time you hear of an environmentalist holding up a plane, I'll be behind the mask.

About the Author

When Yvonne Walus is not a writer, she's a Doctor of Mathematics. A business analyst. A wife and a mother. And always a dreamer who hopes to change the world one book at a time.

Her heritage is inter-continental. The first twelve years of her life in communist Poland taught her not to trust newspapers, how to game the system, to value uniformity, and to ride in public transport squashed between so many people that her feet didn't touch the ground. The next sixteen years in South Africa's apartheid taught her never to trust newspapers, how to game a different system, to value diversity, and to drive the car fifty metres down the road to the mail box. New Zealand is a fantastic country to live in – consequently, she's lived here longer than anywhere else, and she's even beginning to trust newspapers.

Crime fiction is her passion, particularly stories with surprise endings. Her childhood hero was, predictably, Hercule Poirot. Now she loves Harlan Coben's super-rich super-able Win (Windsor Horne Lockwood) and Jack Reacher, but her forever-favourite is Benedict Timothy Carlton Cumberbatch in his role as Sherlock Holmes.

Her website is: www.yvonnewalus.com/

She reviews books on her blog:
   http://yewalus.blogspot.co.nz/

Like to Read More Work Like This?

Then sign up to our mailing list and download our free collection of short stories, *Magnetism*. Sign up now to receive this free e-book and also to find out about all of our new publications and offers.

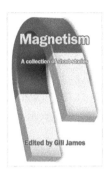

Sign up here:
http://eepurl.com/gbpdVz

Please Leave a Review

Reviews are so important to writers. Please take the time to review this book. A couple of lines is fine.

Reviews help the book to become more visible to buyers. Retailers will promote books with multiple reviews.

This in turn helps us to sell more books… And then we can afford to publish more books like this one.

Leaving a review is very easy.

Go to https://smarturl.it/996t9u, scroll down the left-hand side of the Amazon page and click on the "Write a customer review" button.

Other Books by Yvonne Walus

Serial Wives: Introducing Zero Zimmerman
Published by Stairway Press

Why would a rich girl become a prostitute? Three years ago Joy refused to sleep with an ex boyfriend. When he committed suicide, her guilt was enormous. To punish herself she opted to serve as a prostitute for three years.

How far would you go to protect your child? Cora loves her convict husband despite - or because of - his bad boy ways. But now that he's back in her life, she has their daughter to consider. Is a faulty father better than no father at all?

A serial killer... A serial killer who murders women and displays their bodies dressed in a white sheet with a fencing mask covering the face. Who will be next?

"Strong. Powerful. Engaging. Insightful. These words are not enough to describe this incredible book." (*Amazon*)

Order from Amazon:

Paperback: ISBN 978-1-941071-66-3
eBook: ASIN B07B2RQHGW

Operation: Genocide
Published by Stairway Press

An inhuman agenda… In 1982, Annette Pretorius lives a life of privilege afforded to those of European descent in South Africa, but when her husband is murdered, she discovers a shattering secret: he'd been commissioned by the whites-only South African government to develop a lethal virus aimed at controlling the growth of the black population – already oppressed under the cruel system of apartheid.

A clandestine organization… The murder came with a warning to Annette from a secretive organization: keep our secrets or you too will die. Captain Trevor Watson, Annette's former boyfriend, is appointed to lead the investigation. Watson's loyalty is tested as the evidence stacks against his high-school sweetheart.

And the killing isn't over yet… When the investigation points in a terrifying direction, Annette and Watson face a wrenching choice: protect those they love or sacrifice all to save innocents from racial extermination.

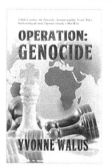

"A true gift to lovers of the thriller genre!" (*Amazon*)

Order from Amazon:
Paperback: ISBN 978-0-984907-07-6
eBook: ASIN B00F8MIJSA

Other Publications by Bridge House

Gatherings
by Mehreen Ahmed

A collection of character based stories, some with a strong element of stream-of-consciousness style.

This book contains twenty-five unthemed short stories. The narratives are picturesque, evocative, and entertaining. They will take the readers on a journey laced with slightly amoral leanings to the serious and in-depth observations of the human condition. With both tragic and comic endings, vices and virtues, entwined into the hearts of the stories, they are all about ordinary people with mundane aspirations, broken dreams, and success.

Gatherings is a single author collection from Bridge House Publishing. Mehreen Ahmed has a well-established voice and is an experienced literary writer.

Order from Amazon:

ISBN: 978-1-914199-02-8 (paperback)
978-1-914199-03-5 (ebook)

Christmas at the Cross
by Maeve Murphy

Blaithnaid's relationship with Kieran is not good. She has allies in Nadina the prostitute who soothes her with potatoes and Yoichi a Japanese neighbour who offers tea but only a little sympathy. David a neighbour supplies something approaching a festive Christmas with plum pudding and White Christmas. There is snow, there are Christmas lights and there are friends meeting for drinks. There is violence, there are threats and there is heartache. How will Blaithnaid find her way through all of this?

Christmas at the Cross – a Kings Cross story – is a novella in five parts from Bridge House Publishing. Maeve Murphy creates a compelling text, an authentic voice and a real sense of place.

"This short novel is gripping, action packed and surprising. Thought provoking and honest. Kings Cross before the face lift." (*Amazon*)

Order from Amazon:

ISBN: 978-1-914199-06-6 (paperback)
978-1-914199-07-3 (ebook)

Speculations
by Stephen Faulkner
What if?

All good stories and novels begin very simply when the author asks the question, "What if…?" In the fourteen stories in Speculations the author offers each solution while leaving it up to you to figure out the "what if…?" question that each tale alludes to.

Each story is an intriguing journey into the realms of imagination, fantasy and the incredible. Some of the places you will be taken in this book include the inner mind of a creature that remains on Earth long after the human race has been eliminated; a world that exports a tasty treat that originates in a quite unsavoury place; and an all-knowing, all powerful alien machine which can do literally anything at all.

Order from Amazon:

ISBN: 978-1-914199-08-0 (paperback)
978-1-914199-09-7 (ebook)